THE LOG

OF THE

JESSIE BILL

THE LOG
OF THE
JESSIE BILL

DEAN GABBERT

M. EVANS
Lanham • Boulder • New York • Toronto • Plymouth, UK

Published by M. Evans
An imprint of Rowman & Littlefield
4501 Forbes Boulevard, Suite 200, Lanham, Maryland 20706
www.rowman.com

10 Thornbury Road, Plymouth PL6 7PP, United Kingdom

Distributed by National Book Network

British Library Cataloguing in Publication Information Available

Library of Congress Cataloging-in-Publication Data

The hardback edition of this book was previously cataloged by the Library of
Congress as follows:

Gabbert, Dean
   The log of the Jessie Bill / Dean Gabbert.
     p. cm. — (An Evans novel of the West)
   1. Young men—Travel—Mississippi—Fiction. 2. Boats and boating—
Mississippi River—Fiction. I. Title. II. Series.
   PS3557.A2245L64   1993
   823'.54—dc20
                       93-28913

ISBN: 978-1-59077-252-2 (pbk. : alk. paper)
ISBN: 978-1-59077-253-9 (electronic)

Printed in the United States of America

Chapter One

I see you are a raftsman, sir,
And not a common bum;
For no one but a raftsman
Stirs coffee with his thumb.

JANUARY 11, 1880:

For the life of me, I don't see how anybody in his right mind would want a berth on a busted down wreck of a boat like the *Jessie Bill*. But then there ain't many people on the *Jessie Bill* in their right minds, if you want to split hairs. Cleve Allen, the second mate, and me are the only ones I can think of, off hand. And even Cleve can get in a terrible sweat when we're standing down the river with a big raft that tries to shave the trees right off the bank and otherwise acts like it was the devil's own property.

There must be better'n 80 raft boats on the Upper Mississippi, but the *Jessie Bill* is in a class all by herself. Honest, you got to see her to believe it. She's so slow she has to work to keep up with the current on a downstream run. Her flues are shot and her engines are more contrary than a government mule. Her chimneys are canted and the last time I counted, she had three busted paddle buckets and maybe six more with bad cracks. Her hog chains ain't strung right and no matter how you load her, she always lists to starboard.

Like ol' Pot Belly, our engineer, says: "The fact that she even floats is a God-damned miracle!"

I'm not one to use cuss words, except in emergencies, and I don't like to put 'em in this log, but there are some things that just don't have the right ring without 'em. Any riverman knows that right off. In fact, most of them are choosey about their cuss words. The best way I know to make a fool out of yourself is to use a wrong cuss word or stick one in where it don't belong. Folks on the bank don't seem to realize that river cussin' is a real art. My Pa used to say there ain't nothin' harder on the ear than the crude cussin' of some landsman.

But before I get clean off the subject, I'd better tell you more about this log and why I'm writin' it. My name's Peter Paul Sherman and I'm mud clerk on the *Jessie Bill*. Flunky might be a better word for it. I'm 17 and if I can live through one more season on this leaky ol' tub, I'll put in for a job on some respectable boat—like the *Fred Weyerhaeuser* or the *J.W. Van Sant*. If you really want the truth, I'm only 15, but I'm big for my age and Pa said it don't hurt to bend the facts a little when it helps you get a job. I guess there's some advantage in comin' from a family of 13 kids; not even the preacher can remember all your names and when it comes to knowin' ages, mostly he don't even come close.

The Shermans ain't much on education, except for me and a couple of sisters. I never had much feeling about school, one way or the other, but Ma figured she had some kind of genius on her hands and that just doubled her determination to make a preacher out of me. I think she got that idea into her head the day I was born. I was the fifth boy and Pa had to put his foot down to keep her from namin' me John Wesley, or maybe it was John Calvin.

I didn't mind goin' to Professor Howe's Academy, except in the spring when the ice went out and the raft boats began to move on the Mississippi. After three or four months of an Iowa winter, there's nothin' like a triple-tone steam whistle to rile your blood and make the shivers go down your back.

I don't want to sound boastful, but I had ol' Prof Howe thinkin' I was a pretty smart kid. The truth was the school was mostly girls and the bulk of them was mighty dumb. What with all the attention I was gettin' from him and my Ma, I could see I was diggin' my own grave with all that book-learnin'. Now I got nothin' against preachers, but bein' one just didn't make sense. If the Good Lord didn't intend for you to be a riverman, why would he let you be born in a town like LeClaire?

Now LeClaire ain't no great shakes of a town, but it's mighty serious about the river. If there's a place on the Upper Mississippi that's got more rivermen per square foot, I wish somebody'd tell me about it. If it wasn't for LeClaire's pilots, there'd be a sight more wrecks clutterin' up the Rock Island Rapids, too. The rapids start right here and run most of the way to Davenport. Right at 15 miles. If you was to show them to a landsman, he'd probably laugh at you, but it's those crazy rocks on the bottom that put the fear of the Lord into a steamboatman. They call 'em chains and they run every which way with only a narrow, winding channel to keep you out of trouble. Every chain is different from the next and the whole puzzle changes with each stage of water.

We've got five or six pilots in LeClaire, like Mike Clarke and Jeremy Johnson, who do nothin' but run the rapids. Specialists, the professor calls 'em. For 25 dollars they'll take a 600-foot raft through without peelin' the bark off a single log. The oldtimers claim that Clarke once took a light draft packet down to Davenport when the early-morning dew on the bank was deeper'n the water in the river.

Some of the biggest men on the river got their start in LeClaire, but the town just sort of takes them for granted. The womenfolk like to brag about James Eads and Will Cody as if they was the only natives who ever 'mounted to more'n a hill of beans. Eads was a famous engineer who built a lot of bridges. Mostly, riverman don't have any truck with bridge people, but the town was willin' to overlook it in his case. Eads knew the river and he knew boats. It was his gunboats, in fact, that opened the Mississippi during the war and helped the North lick the South. That's a heap more'n you can say for Buffalo Bill Cody. He left here when he was a kid, and as far as I know, he's never been back. What's so hot about shootin' wild cows out in Kansas an' traveling around the country with a bunch of Indians puttin' on tent shows? I always figured he was some kind of traitor.

Ever since I was big enough to know the difference between a jackstaff and a sounding pole, I figured on following the river. When you've got four brothers who're all steamboatman, your mind just sort of runs in that direction. Christian—he's the oldest—is already makin' a name for hisself on the lower river. Right now he's relief .pilot on the *J. M. White* and I guess that gives him the right to be uppity and wear dude clothes when he comes home. If you've never heard of the *White*, then you don't know much about riverboats. She's the biggest and fastest packet on the Mississippi, and as far as I know, the only one with French chandeliers in her main salon. Brother Matthew is first mate on the *Prairie State* out of Dubuque and Mark and Luke are both rousters on the *Jeannie Deans,* an old sidewheeler that runs in the Quincy and St. Louis trade.

Then there was Pa, rest his cantankerous old soul. Sometimes I think he hated the river, but he could never leave it alone. He was born in Indiana and he went to work on a keelboat when he was just a little shaver, back in the '40s. He shipped lead out of Galena before the mines petered out and when he and Ma was first married, he ran a lightering boat on the Des Moines Rapids below Montrose.

I suppose I'd better stop right here and tell you what a lightering boat is, or else you'll think I'm making things up. The Des Moines Rapids was just like the Rock Island Rapids, only worse. About half the time the bigger boats couldn't get through without stovin' in their hulls, so they started building ugly little flat-bottom jobs with hardly no draft at all. Upstream boats would unload part of their freight at Keokuk and the flat-bottoms would haul it to Montrose where another boat would take it aboard and head upriver. One summer the river got down to a bare trickle and the lightering had to be done overland. When Pa heard they wanted to make a mule-skinner out of him, he grabbed Ma and the one or two kids they had then and started north. He finally quit cussin' when they got to LeClaire and that's where the Sherman clan has been ever since. Pa wasn't the only one who took an unkindly view of those rapids and all the trouble they caused. The government frittered around for years tryin' to figure out what to do and they finally dug a canal along the Iowa shore and put in three locks. Now the packets go through without wettin' a sounding pole. But it's hard to get three acres of logs through a canal, so us poor raftsmen mostly fight the rocks and shoals and swear at the government for playin' favorites.

Pa had his own raft boat about the time I was born, but he lost it in the ice a few years later and from then on nothin' seemed to go right. He knew logs and lumber as well as he knew steamboats, but the fight went out of him when he busted his leg while tryin' to round up a runaway raft up near the mouth of the Wisconsin River. He was owly and bitter around the house and after he started hittin' the bottle, most captains wouldn't hire him on a bet. It made me sick seein' him sittin' around the Green Tree Hotel day after day waitin' for a boat that needed a hand. The Green Tree Hotel ain't a hotel at all; it's a big ol' elm tree down by the landing. Professor Howe figures it's been there for 125 years and maybe longer. It's sort of a landmark on the river and when a man's lookin' for a berth, he throws his kit under the tree and sets up housekeepin' until the right boat comes along.

I guess you could say Pa and me never did hit it off too well. He had us older kids pretty much buffaloed, but not Ma, and that's why he never said too much against me bein' a preacher. Finally I got so big it wore him out every time he had to whip me and he decided it was time I went to the river. As far as I know, that was the only time we ever agreed on anything.

The biggest problem was gettin' out of Howe's Academy. About the only way, I decided, was to be throwed out for misconduct. It's a funny thing, but some kids can get themselves into a heap of trouble without battin' an eye; then the next one can do everything from suckin' eggs to burnin' down barns and never get caught. Anyway, I worked at it. I nailed down the lids in the girls toilet; I dropped a dead mouse in the water bucket; and I put a board over the chimney, smokin' up the school and causin' the professor to have such a fit of coughing that he busted his upper plate. But nothin' did any good. Every time I confessed, he licked somebody else.

If it hadn't been for the professor's daughter, Petunia, I reckon I'd be there yet. Mr. Howe called her Pet. She was a couple years older'n me and about as friendly as a polecat—at first, that is. Her ma was dead and she did the cookin' and cleanin' for her pa and helped him teach the lower grades. She looked like a Petunia, too—about two days after a killin' frost. Her spectacles were thick as a whisky bottle and her teeth were about right for eatin' roastin' ears through a picket fence.

I aimed to stay as far away from her as I could get, until one day I made what you might call a discovery: as long as you didn't look at her face, there was something about the rest of her that made you feel sort of warm inside. I guess you'd call it her shape; I knew it had all of a sudden changed for the better. For one thing, her shirtwaist was mighty full in front and when she'd dance with the second grade, I was always scared she'd pop her buttons right in the middle of the Virginia Reel. But the thing that got me the most was that funny little wiggle she had when she walked. I don't know how she did it exactly, but I have to admit it was fun to watch.

One day she dropped her pencil as she was passing my desk, and when she bent over to pick it up my hand went snakin' out—with me hardly knowin' what it was doing—and pinched her rear. I could feel the blood risin' under my collar and I waited for her scream that I knew was going to take the roof right off the school. But so help me, she never uttered a word—not one peep. Instead, she looked around sly like and winked her eye!

Now I got a flock of sisters, and while one'll fool you sometimes, I can pretty much tell how a female is going to act. But I never run into one like this before. How was I to know that some girls like to have their butts pinched?

Anyway, from that day on it was like havin' a private tutor. Those poor little second and third graders didn't stand a chance. Petunia was right there every minute, leanin' over my desk to check my work. Casting eyes at her from a distance is one thing, but feelin' those strainin' buttons against the side of your head is somethin' else, let me tell you. It wasn't long until the other kids began to get wise and even the professor could see that Petunia was fast makin' a fool out of herself.

One evening when I was doin' chores, I saw Howe's buggy tied out in front and I knew somethin' was up. Ma told me about it later. After three cups of tea and a half a batch of cookies, he got around to Petunia and me. He gnawed around the subject for a while longer and then he said we had a bad case of puppy love and ought to be separated to prevent any unfortunate developments. The best solution, he allowed, was for me to quit school and get a job on the river.

Now Ma ain't one to beat around the bush. She sat me down after supper and began hittin' me over the head with a lot of silly questions about Petunia. I wasn't givin' her very straight answers, because I didn't want to spoil the professor's story. Then she comes right out and asks: "Have you got that girl in a family way? At your age?"

Well, that just about knocked me for a loop. I wasn't too well versed in the facts of life then, but I knew that gettin' a gal in a family way involved a heap more than a pinch on the back side. I jumped up and gave her a loud "No, mam!" Then I stomped out of the room like I was havin' a fit of temper. She must have felt a little sheepish about it, because she didn't call me back.

The next day ol' Howe was all peaches 'n cream. It was time I got a job, he said, and he knew just the riverboat that would take me on. I was eatin' up every word of it until he mentioned the *Jessie Bill*. Every kid in this town knows there's not a sorrier vessel between here and St. Louis. I felt like tellin' him I'd rather marry his homely daughter and teach school than work on that ol' tub, but then he tells me he's one of the owners! That was more'n I could take.

"It's all settled, Peter," he says. "The *Jessie Bill* needs a mud clerk and all I have to do is say the word."

I couldn't see no way out, so I gave him a sickly smile and told him I'd take it. Then he tells me he doesn't want people to know he owns part of the *Jessie Bill*. I could understand that all right, but he said it had something to do with his job at the school.

He kept ramblin' on and the next thing I knew he was offering me a five-dollar gold piece at the end of the season if I'd keep a log for him while I was on the boat. He said he wanted the information for some history paper he was preparing, but I figured it was just a sneaky way to spy on the captain.

As you can probably guess, he was short of cash when the time came and I'm glad it turned out that way. After lookin' over last year's notes, I've decided they're worth a sight more than a measly five bucks. Heck, the crazy things that happen on the *Jessie Bill* are a lot wilder than the stuff you read about in dime novels. Even if I stuck to the truth and didn't dress it up none, I know I could make a pile of money once I got hooked up with one of those eastern publishers.

But I'm gettin' way ahead of my story again. After the professor stepped in, Ma began to weaken some, but she still wasn't convinced I was cut out to be a riverman. I kept chippin' away at her pretty hard and when the news came about Pa, she finally gave in.

Lige Holloway brought us the word one evening at suppertime. He was all out of breath and his eyes were bugged out something fierce. It took a long time to get the story out of him.

The *John C. North* needed a mate for a run to Quincy and Pa took the job. She grounded on a bar near the Illinois side above New Boston and Frank Caldwell, the captain, tried to walk her off. He called for steam and he got it—all in one big blast. Pa was standin' near the port chimney when the boilers blew. Some farmer found his body in a cornfield 50 feet from the bank.

They brought him home in a pine box the next day, all black and swelled up like a poisoned pup. All I could do was lean on the lid and bawl.

Chapter Two

One doesn't hit a rock or
a solid log raft with a steam-
boat when he can get excused.
—Mark Twain

MARCH 18, 1880:

Captain Lafayette Clapsaddle is just the kind of a master you'd expect to find on the *Jessie Bill*. In a way, they sort of resemble each other, both bein' in a run-down condition and a little frayed around the edges.

A name like Lafayette would be a burden to most people, but not the captain. I've heard it said he likes to sign papers just for the fun of spillin' those loops and curlycues all over the page. As far as I know, his wife is the only soul who calls him by his given name. When she booms out "Lafayette" in that deep voice of hers, it makes me think of George Washington and the Revolutionary War.

River folks don't let a man put on airs for long and the captain hadn't been in LeClaire for a month when they chopped his fancy handle down to plain ol' Lafe. This rankled him, it did indeed. He fought it, but in the end it didn't do no good.

Our roustabouts got some other names for him, too, but I never heard one you could print. Once in a while Four-Mile Freeman—he's the first mate—will call him 'ol Saddlesore right to his face, but the captain always lets on like he didn't hear it.

I'd guess the captain to be about 48 or 50—give or take a few years. He's short and kind of dumpy and if you looked at him twice, it'd be because of his ears. Honest, they stick out like paddleboxes on a sidewheel packet. You couldn't say he was cross-eyed, but he's got one eye that doesn't always track right. His nose is red in the summertime and blue in the winter. There's nothin' but bare skin on the top of his head with a fringe of red hair on the sides and some scraggly mutton-chop whiskers growin' on the underside of his jaw. His chin sort of gives up right below his bottom lip and the rest of the way it's all neck.

When he's ashore or when we got visitors aboard, the captain always flashes his gold teeth and gives everybody a lot of honey talk. He's a great one for shakin' hands with important-looking people. Then he pats 'em on the back and the next thing you know he's got an arm around their shoulder. I never will forget that day last summer when he patted the Widow Dailey in the wrong place and she liked to drove him through the boiler deck with her umbrella. It took Bush McDonald and me both to pry his beaver hat off his ears.

Any steamboat master worth his salt will have things shipshape and ready to go at least a month before the ice goes out. Not Cap'n Lafe, though. Last year the *Menominee* had been all the way to Beef Slough and was comin' down with the season's first raft before the *Jessie Bill* ever got away from the landing. She always winters with two or three other stray boats in Lyman's Slough at the mouth of Brush Creek. You could pick her out a half-mile away by her dirty-gray color and down-at-the-mouth appearance. There's one stanchion missing on the port side and her deck railing has never been fixed since that time she bumped the *Enterprise* while tryin' to make a landing at Dallas City.

Cleve Allen said he's heard she was a pretty fair boat in her day, but that must have been a powerful long time ago. She's 125 feet long with a 22$\frac{1}{2}$-foot beam and a 3-foot hold. The captain claims she draws only 28 inches light, but that don't allow for a ton or two of water that's usually sloshin' around in her hold. Her hull has so many cracks in it that it takes a couple of barrels of oakum a year to keep her from sinkin'. Her boilers have got patches on the patches and you wouldn't believe her engines. How something with only a 14-inch bore and a four-foot stroke can make that much racket is beyond me.

I reckon I could fill a whole logbook just tellin' about our crew. They can cuss louder, drink more rot-gut, get in more fights and do more gold-brickin' than any rafting outfit on the river. Four-Mile says most of 'em are pretty good at wenching, too. Some are dumber than others and there's a few who would choose a lickin' over a bath any day. One or two get a little careless about payin' for things when they go ashore, but I wouldn't want you to think we had any criminals aboard. Mudcat Lewis— he's second fireman—did a hitch in the state penitentiary at Fort Madison for stealin' a flatboat full of chickens, but he said it never would have happened if he'd had a fair trial and if the judge hadn't been biased just because they was his uncle's chickens.

Some raftboats have a crew of 18 or so, counting the captain and the pilot. The *J. W. Van Sant*, which is about the best rafter in these parts, has two engineers, two firemen, two mates and at least seven rousters. Then there's the cook and his helper, the clerk and a couple of watchmen who operate the steam nigger and take care of the handyman jobs.

Believe me, that would be a real crowd on the *Jessie Bill*. Once in a while we can muster 14 hands, but most of the time it'd be hard to round up an even dozen. I guess there ain't too many raftin' men who can stand bad grub and bad pay all at the same time. Mostly, it takes a small mutiny to get wages out of the captain. Even then, it's usually one part money and two part promises.

I never seen a man who had as many money problems as Lafe Clapsaddle. He's got debts like a dog has fleas; every year he has to go further away from home to borrow money. But I got to hand it to him—he always manages to scrounge a little here and there with his fast talk and smart-soundin' propositions.

Ol' Pot Belly—his real name is Oakley Carmichael, only nobody hardly ever calls him that—is all the time goin' on about the captain's finances. In fact, that and Mrs. Carmichael's cussedness and contrary disposition are the two things he talks about most.

"Now you take a spendthrift," he says, pokin' me with one of those big oilcans, "he's a man you could almost admire because he's throwing around his own money. But that ain't what Lafe Clapsaddle does. No siree, Bob! He blows somebody else's money. And you know what that makes him? A dad-burned deadbeat, that's what!"

If Cap'n Lafe has got any special talent, you'd have to say it was dodgin' creditors. Lord knows, there's a heap of 'em to dodge. It's downright uncanny the way he can disappear when one shows up. Four-Mile Freeman says he can smell a creditor up to a mile away. I know that ain't so because last fall we put in at Trempealeau on our way upriver and the captain's nose wasn't too good that day. He was in a big rush to get ashore and when he came back, some skinny little guy in a linen suit came sneakin' along behind him and made it up the stageplank before we could cast off.

He kept askin' for the captain and when nobody'd give him a straight answer, he just stood there on the front end twistin' his hat in his hands and gettin' madder by the minute. Pretty soon I saw a man come down from the boiler deck wearing a long coat and a black hat that was about two sizes too big. He had on one of those Roman collars and was holdin' a Bible in his hands. I had to look twice before I realized it was the captain.

He walked right up to the skinny fellow and grabbed him by the arm and said, "Praise God, you must be the doctor."

The guy pulled back and cocked his head. "Doctor? I ain't no doctor."

The captain grabbed him again. "But you must be. I've given those poor sick men last rites and there's nothing more I can do."

By now our visitor was back-trackin' toward the plank. "Who's sick? What they got?"

"Smallpox, my good man. That's why we sent for you. One poor soul has passed to his reward. I'm afraid the other two won't last until morning."

I don't reckon that guy heard more'n the first word. He hit the bank at a full gallop and he hadn't slacked off a bit when he crossed the levee and went out of sight. You should've heard Four-Mile laugh. Tears rolled down his face and he had an awful time catchin' his breath. "There you seen it, Peter Paul boy," he gasped. "The greatest piece of acting since Edwin Booth."

It was funny alright, but I never did figure out where the captain got that crazy collar.

Cap'n Lafe is the only temperance man I know who gets drunk at least once a month. Not roarin' drunk like Ercel Waters or Limber Jim Gray, but just quiet-drunk. If you'd ask him, he'd probably swear on a stack of Bibles that he's never been drunk in his life. Oh, he hates whisky like the plague and wouldn't take a drop of it if he was dyin' of thirst. But he's got a weakness for wine—and it don't matter what kind or what color.

Pot Belly says some quack doctor down at Davenport told the captain once that a little wine was good for the heart and he must've figured right there that he was never going to have any heart trouble. Anyway, he's got wine hid around all over the boat. Once the rousters found two gallons of pistingle—the kind you make out of rhubarb—tucked away in the rope locker and it was goin' on 12 hours before Four-Mile got a lick of work out of 'em.

By the middle of February, we had about half a crew on board tryin' to get ready for the spring break-up. Pot Belly and Four-Mile was doin' what they could but we weren't makin' much headway—mainly because we didn't have any of what the captain calls working capital.

Lafe, he took off about the first of the month and said he'd be back in a week, but it was the 17th before he showed up, ridin' a borrowed horse and showin' a big smile. He'd been clear to Cedar Rapids and from the careful way he handled the saddlebags, I figured that was a far piece to go just for a fresh supply of wine. But he also had some cash and a couple of letters of credit and right away he started talkin' about how much money we was going to make this year—if the boat hung together and we all worked hard.

The ice started to go out on March 3rd and by the 5th the channel was pretty much open. Pot Belly finally got the mud pump to work and Four-Mile rounded up two new deckhands to replace those who quit last fall. The *Stillwater* and the *Borealis Rex* moved out of Lyman's Slough on the 6th and by that time we was all gettin' fidgety. Every riverman in LeClaire was watchin' the weather and the ice and keepin' his ears open for reports of conditions upstream. All the saloons were already takin' bets on what LeClaire boat would be the first to reach Beef Slough. Being the first boat to leave the landing is something to brag about; but it don't mean you'll bring down the first raft. Not by a long shot.

Everybody still talks about the *Muscatine Belle* and the *Silver Swan* back in '74. Their captains was big rivals and a couple of know-it-alls to boot. They both wanted that first raft and they pulled away from the landing like they was the *Natchez* and the *Robert E. Lee.* They ran bow to stern until a blizzard hit them at Dunleith, and from then on it was pure hell. Neither one would quit, though, until the ice caught them in Betsey Slough Bend five miles above Winona. A week later the *Muscatine Belle* heeled over and sunk under a big gorge and the *Silver Swan* was laid up most of the season gettin' her hull patched up. You can bet the *Jessie Bill* will never get caught in any scrapes like that, not as long as Lafe Clapsaddle is in charge. I wouldn't say the captain is chicken-hearted, but he's not one to take chances— maybe with somebody else's money, but not with his own hide.

We'd had steam up for two days, but the captain kept stallin' and I knew he didn't want to move until our pilot, Wabasha Dan Wilson, was aboard. Now Wabasha Dan is just about as independent as a hog on ice. There's not another pilot on the river who's half as bull-headed and half as cantankerous. We knew he'd show up when he was good and ready, but we couldn't see the sense of waitin' around when we could be down at the LeClaire landing takin' on fuel and provisions.

You maybe won't believe this, but it's an honest fact that the captain's got no stomach for piloting. Like Cleve Allen says, he hasn't got a pilot's feel; the harder he tries the worse he gets. When he's at the helm, everybody just sort of hunches their back and waits for somethin' to happen. If there's anything in the river or over the river to hit, there's a good chance he'll do it.

A few raft boats carry two pilots, but mostly the captain and one pilot spell each other at the wheel. Only it don't work that way on the *Jessie Bill.* No, sir. The only time Cap'n Lafe goes near the pilothouse is when Wabasha Dan is on a bender or when he needs a little sleep. If the weather turns bad or if there's a tricky crossing comin' up, like as not he'll pretend he's sick and tie up until Dan is ready to take over.

But this time the captain got tired of waitin' and on the morning of the 10th he told me to hoof it to town and start roundin' up stores. I had a list as long as your arm of everything we needed, but by the time he got done scratchin' off this and addin' that, I could hardly read it. Like always, I had to ask him what I was supposed to use for money. He dug some out of his pouch and then he gave me a big lecture about the world being overrun with smart-alec steamboat clerks. Let me tell you, that man can be a trial.

I wanted to go to the livery stable and rent a dray, but he had it all fixed up for me to borrow Professor Howe's team and wagon. I didn't argue none because I could see a free breakfast and a chance to find out if Petunia still had that funny little wiggle-walk. Pa used to say there are days when a man's a damn fool for ever gettin' out of bed and that day was one of 'em. In the first place, breakfast was over by the time I made the Howe place and all I got was a half-cold cup of coffee and a lot of silly chatter from Petunia.

Then things got worse when the professor told me Petunia would go to town with me and bring the team and wagon home. That was bad enough, but the ol' boy was huddled up to the stove all loaded with goose grease and camphorated oil and I could see he was in no shape to harness up those two spavined mares of his.

So Petunia and I lit out for the carriage house with me tryin' to figure out how I was going to attach a team of horses to a wagon without lettin' that gabby female know I didn't have the slightest idea how to do it. I took a horse collar off its peg since that seemed like a logical place to start and I was tryin' to decide which was the top and which was the bottom, when she hit me in the face with her rabbit-fur muff an' told me to step aside.

It's a good thing I did, too, because she whizzed around the stall throwin' leather like a California wagonmaster. I got red in the face the first time she reached for a crupper, but she lifted that horse's tail and slapped it in place without battin' an eye.

Then she popped on the bridles and the next thing I knew she had 'em outside hookin' the tugs to the singletrees.

I don't mind sayin' my mouth was still hangin' open when we climbed into the seat. She snatched her muff back, tossed me the reins and said "Hoist the anchor, Captain Ahab. Full speed ahead." I swear, that windy woman says anything that pops into her head, and mostly it don't make sense.

We'd barely got started when she reached under the seat and pulled out a moth-eaten ol' lap robe and piled it around us like it was the dead of winter. You'd of thought she was freezin' the way she kept crowdin' up against me until we both didn't hardly take up half the seat. Then she started asking questions. I mean stupid questions.

"Don't you ever get seasick on the river?"

Before I could answer, she had a couple more.

"Aren't you frightened when you have to climb way up to the crow's nest on a stormy night?"

Right then I knew where she got that Captain Ahab stuff. She'd been reading *Moby Dick* and she thought we spent our time chasin' whales up an' down the Mississippi in four-masted schooners. That's how dumb she was!

I was gettin' desperate when we reached the edge of town and I liked to wore out the buggy whip trying to put that team into a trot, but those rump-sprung ol' mares just kept ploddin' along like they was leading a funeral procession. Finally I just pulled my cap down over my eyes and prayed nobody'd recognize me.

All the time I kept thinkin' I'd be shut of Petunia as soon as we reached Main Street, but I was wrong there, too. I couldn't get more'n two steps ahead of her all morning long; everytime I told her I thought she should go visit her sick Aunt Emma, she just laughed. That girl can stick to a body like glue. It didn't matter whose store I was in, she was right there under foot. And that mouth of hers was flappin' all the time, tellin' me to buy this and not buy that. What a botheration!

Outfitting a steamboat ain't no easy job, even when you're not playin' nursemaid to an addled female. Along about the third load I was fair tuckered out, and hungry, too. I had a mountain of stuff piled at the lower landing below Carlson's wharfboat, but by then that woman had me so confused I didn't know whether I was comin' or goin'. Then to top it off, I lost my list and there was nothin' to do but try and finish the job from memory.

The last load was mostly hardware, except for two barrels of molasses and a tub of salt pork. By the time I paid for two reels of three-quarter check line and an assortment of axes, crank augers, pike poles, snatch poles and peavies, I didn't have enough silver left for as much as a box of snuff. Not that I wanted any snuff, you understand. I tried some once and took the cure, right there. Freeman had told me to get a supply of plugs and lockdowns for raft repairs, but I figured he could make some, his being pretty handy when it comes to riggin' up something out of nothing.

I did buy Petunia a bag of lemon drops after she hinted several times. About the middle of the afternoon it looked like that was about all the dinner we was going to get. If I'd had any money of my own, I might have taken her over to Ma Jones' Hash House. But I never invited a woman out to eat in my life and I figured I'd better not start on Captain Lafe's money.

I was thinkin' how I could sneak some bread and cheese out of the galley without Fatback—he's our cook—seein' me when I spotted the *Jessie Bill* comin' 'round the point above town. I let off unloading the rest of the gear right then because those lazy rousters hadn't turned a hand all day and I knew Four-Mile would be lookin' for ways to keep 'em out of mischief.

There wasn't an uncommon lot of traffic that day, but enough boats was movin' in and out of the landing to keep a pilot from going to sleep. The *Jessie Bill* was creeping along slow-like, holding to the bank. I could see the *Jayhawker* heading upriver with the *Crescent City* tailing along behind and angling inland like she was going to land somewheres behind the *Jessie Bill*. The *Lucky Lucy* was tied up near the Duncan place with a full head of steam and when all of a sudden she started backin' out, I knew there was going to be trouble.

Captain Lafe hung on the whistle cord for quite a spell and then he must have laid the wheel over to port as far as it'd go. Now the *Jessie Bill* is what some call a slow responder. She swung out all right and missed the *Lucy*'s stern with plenty to spare, but she took her sweet time about comin' back and that's when the pilot of the *Crescent City* started blowin' his whistle and ringin' his engine bell all at the same time.

First I shut my eyes, but when I heard the sound of wood splittin' wood, I had to look. There was the *Jessie Bill*'s bow ridin' up over the *Crescent City*'s guard about midship on the port side. Busted deck stanchions was pointin' in all directions and what was left of the *Jessie*'s jackstaff looked to be only a foot or two from the *Crescent City*'s nearest boiler. For an instant there was dead silence. Then the engine bells began clangin' again and people started swarmin' around on both boats, yellin' and cussin' and wavin' their arms like crazy. The racket sort of reminded me of the time at home when our tomcat got shut in the henhouse.

The *Crescent City* is a rafter like the *Jessie Bill*, only a little bigger and a lot newer. I could tell she got the worst of it when the two boats started to swing in a slow circle with the current. The *Crescent* is owned by Erin Murphy, a hot-headed Irishman and one of those lightning pilots who's always lookin' for a race. He was leanin' out of the pilothouse and I knew he was readin' Cap'n Clapsaddle's pedigree like Lafe'd never heard it done before.

After a time everybody got tired of jawin' and started tryin' to figure out how to get out of their predicament without doin' more damage. Finally they both started backin' slow-like. There was a lot of creakin' and groanin' and then the *Jessie Bill*'s nose pulled free and went down with a splash. I thought she was a goner, but her bow came up and she limped on down to the landing with only a couple of new scars to go with all her old ones. Freeman just looked at me and shook his head when I came up the plank to try and hustle some grub for me and Petunia. There wasn't any smoke comin' out of his ears, but it wouldn't have surprised me none if there had been. He sent Limber Jim Gray off to cut a new jackstaff and the other rousters, not wantin' to get Four-Mile any madder'n he already was, started bringin' on supplies without being told.

Petunia finally shamed me into waterin' the horses and I was standing there with a bucket lettin' one of those mares slobber all over me when the storm hit. Only this storm didn't have anything to do with the weather. All the wind was comin' from that Irishman Murphy as he stomped up to the stageplank and demanded cash damages for his boat. Then he let go with a few more names for Cap'n Clapsaddle that he must have thought up along the way. Right behind him was the crew of the *Crescent City,* every last one of 'em spoilin' for trouble.

It's times like those when the captain knows how to make himself scarce. Murphy took a couple of steps up the plank, threw back his head and bellered like a bull: "Where are you, Clapsaddle? You'll give us satisfaction right here and now or we'll take apart this miserable excuse of a boat board by board!"

"What kind of satisfaction you lookin' for?" It was Freeman talkin' as he came down from the boiler deck three steps at a time. Now Four-Mile is a man who just naturally commands respect. And that goes double when his dander's up. He stands six-foot-three in his bare feet and when he throws out his chest and draws up those arms, he's about as peaceful lookin' as a grizzly bear.

Murphy was carryin' an ax handle and he made his first mistake when he shook it at Freeman. Quick as a cat, Four-Mile grabbed the Irishman like a sack of meal and flung him across his shoulder. Then he gave a mighty heave and Murphy hit the water belly-first, kickin' and cussin'. The rest of those *Crescent City* cut-throats swarmed up the plank and pitched into Freeman before he could get turned around. It was gettin' crowded on the forecastle by the time Cleve Allen and Grumble Jones, the first fireman, and Mudcat Lewis got there; all I could see from the bank was swingin' arms, legs and pike poles.

Ol' Pot Belly cooled one of the invaders with a stick of firewood and then Ercel Waters vaulted over the boiler deck rail and dropped right into the middle of the pile, whoopin' like a wild Indian. About that time the whole mess of 'em came rollin' down the plank and spilled out across the landing.

In a minute or so some of the *Crescent City* boys spotted our supplies and that put Petunia and me and those bay mares right in the middle of the melee. Limber Jim and our two new rousters, Argonaut Smith and Pinhead Grant, slowed 'em up some and I tagged one good and proper with a water bucket.

Before I could climb up in the wagon to protect Petunia, she kicked one fellow in the back of the head and cracked another *Crescent City* skull with the butt end of her buggy whip. It was the most unlady-like spectacle I've ever seen. There she was smackdab in the middle of a riverfront brawl, swingin' that whip and yellin' like a banshee! I looked a little too long and the next thing I knew I was on my back with a busted lip. I'd hardly more'n got back on my feet when I got hit from two different directions by a bag of salt and a side of bacon. They didn't hurt none, but it was plain that our summer's supply of grub was gettin' sore abused.

Bush McDonald went chargin' past me with both fists swingin' at nothin' in particular. Then I spotted ol' Fatback out on the fringe with a stove poker in his hand tryin' to figure out who was friend and who was foe. I gave him a wide berth, because a man who ain't able to see past the end of his nose can do more harm then good when it comes to fightin'. Things were going our way after Freeman and Grumble Jones started workin' as a team, but then a bunch of strangers jumped in just for the fun of it, not givin' a hang whose side they was on. I was gettin' up for the third time when a couple of johnny-come-latelys slammed against the wagon and scared the daylights out of Petunia's team. They snorted off down the levee before she could grab the reins and those molasses barrels came flying out the back end. They popped like pumpkins when they hit the cobblestones and all of a sudden the whole place was ankle-deep in molasses with a bunch of flour thrown in for good measure.

If I live to be 100, I never expect to see such slippin' and slidin'! It was the granddaddy of all messes! Some were on their backs and some were on their bellies, lookin' like hogs in a wallow. I was sort of in between and I didn't know whether to laugh or cry. One thing sure, when that stuff starts gettin' in your eyes and your nose, it takes the fight out of you. While everybody was tryin' to get to dry ground, the fire bell began to ring. There wasn't no smoke to be seen and I figured Marshal Raintree was callin' out the Volunteer Fire Department to break up the brawl. Raintree's old and crotchety, but he's still handy with a gun full of birdshot.

The bell was still ringin' when the *Jessie Bill*'s whistle blew—
loud and urgent. Every man-jack member of the crew knew in an
instant it was Wabasha Dan on that cord, blowin' a highball and
tellin' the whole town he was pullin' out. There's not a man on
the river who can make a whistle talk like that. It never dawned
on a soul that there was no one aboard to answer the engine bells
or hoist the plank; you just know that when Dan blows for a
departure, you'd better jump. Nobody knew where he'd been or
how he got on board, but they all started runnin'—everybody but
me, that is. There I stood, drippin' blood and molasses, wonderin' where Petunia was and how I was going to get her and
those two beasts home. The *Crescent City* bums and a few of
those other hoodlums stood around and jeered for a spell, but as
soon as the marshal and a half dozen firemen hove into view,
they scattered.

The marshal hollered and fired his 12-gauge in the air, but
they didn't pay him no heed. He also ordered the *Jessie Bill* back
to the landing, but all he got was a nose thumbing from Bush
McDonald. About that time he spotted me, up near the top of the
landing, minding my own business. "Arrest that culprit!" he
bawled, all the time grabbin' firemen and pointin' 'em in my
direction.

I was tryin' to decide which way to run when I saw Petunia
and those fool mares coming hell-bent up the levee from the
south. There she was standin' behind the seat with her hair flying' every which-way, swingin' her whip and lookin' for all the
world like a Roman chariot driver! As soon as she saw the trouble I was in, she swung the wagon between two big piles of
freight and headed straight for the firemen. Man, how they did
scramble. I dived for the tailgate as she flew past, and after
hangin' by my fingernails for most of a block, I finally got
myself inside that wild-jumpin' wagon.

How a pair of nags that looked like they escaped from the
glue factory could run like that, I don't guess I'll ever know.
They went through town at a dead gallop and they hardly let up
until we turned into the Howes' gate. It was beginning to get
dark and all I wanted to do was get out of there before Professor
Howe got a look at his daughter. What with her hair undone and

her face all smudged up, she looked like she had tangled with a bobcat. I mumbled something about helpin' her unhitch the team, but she wouldn't hear to it. Then there was a long silence while I tried to pick out the right words to tell her how I admired her for standin' up to those hoodlums. I barely got started when she grabbed me 'round the neck and kissed me, split lip and all! If I hadn't been so surprised, I think I might have enjoyed it. 'Specially since I couldn't see that homely face.

Chapter Three

Pushing mighty hard, boys,
Sandbar's in the way;
Working like a son-of-a-gun
For mighty scanty pay.

APRIL 3, 1880:

I don't know what the penalty is for jail-breakin', but I reckon I'll find out the next time Marshal Raintree gets his hands on me. I had every intention of bustin' out of his calaboose, but when it come to wreckin' the place, that was strictly an accident.

After takin' Petunia home, I hot-footed it back to town and started huntin' for an upstream boat that could help me catch up with the *Jessie Bill*. She didn't have much wood and I knew ol' Fatback would be screamin' his head off if he didn't get more supplies to replace those we lost at the landing. I spotted the *LeClaire Belle* by the outline of her chimneys against the sky and I was fixin' to hail the nightwatchman when a dark shape stepped out from the corner of the wharfboat and wrapped two cold hands around my throat. I was too scared to holler until I found out it was the marshal, then I hollered all the way to the jail.

"What're you pickin' on me for?" I kept asking, but I never got a straight answer. Then I reminded him that out of about 30 grown men, the only one he could catch was an innocent mud clerk who hadn't done a thing all afternoon except try to keep from gettin' killed. I could tell it was gettin' his goat and as soon as he shoved me in the cell and couldn't get his hands on me, I started callin' for my constitutional rights. I didn't know exactly what my rights was, but it was plain I wasn't gettin' 'em. When I demanded to know the charges against me, he exploded.

"Inciting a riot, engaging in an affray, malicious mischief and resisting arrest!" he roared. Then he rattled off three or four more offenses, includin' sassin' an officer of the law. "For that you ain't getting a bite of supper," he said as he stomped out and slammed the door behind him.

What everybody calls the jail is really the Town Hall, a dilapidated two-story building that's put together sort of like the Leaning Tower of Pisa. There's a big round oak table where the town council meets and a little cubbyhole off to one side for the marshal. There's a jail cell big enough to hold a cot in one end and store two voting booths in the other. The fire company hose cart is kept in the back and there's an outside stairway that leads to the marshal's quarters on the second floor.

Bein' pretty disgusted with the whole day, I flopped down on the cot—and promptly ended up on the floor when the head legs gave way. The blamed thing was held together with nothin' but wire—and that gave me a big, beautiful idea! Over on the west wall was a hutch cupboard, doctored up some to hold the marshal's guns. And on the side of the cupboard, not more'n 10 feet away, was a big brass key hanging on a nail.

The marshal—bless his black heart—left a lamp burnin' near the front door and there was just enough light to see while I unwound the wire from the cot and carefully straightened out all the twists and kinks. For a minute, I thought it was too short. But by stickin' my arm and some of my shoulder between the bars, I could just barely reach the cupboard. There was just one trouble; the danged wire was too limber. I kept fishin', though, and after about 15 minutes I knocked the key off the nail. Then I quick-like put a hook in the end of the wire and in another two minutes I had myself a key. And it worked, too. That cell lock turned without so much as a squeak.

I started to slip out the back way, then I decided I'd outsmart the marshal and unload his guns, just in case he missed me before I got too far away. There was three pieces in the rack: a double-barreled shotgun, a Winchester carbine and a Springfield muzzle-loader that looked like it was left over from the Battle of Bull Run. Unloading the first two was easy, but that ol' blunderbuss had me stumped. The thing weighed a ton and the barrel looked almost big enough to drop a cat down. Finally I got it figured out: lift the hammer, take the percussion cap off the nipple and there's no way in the world it can be fired.

The only trouble was I didn't quite get it done. I lifted the hammer all right, but my thumb slipped before I got it cocked and that undersized cannon went off with a thunderclap. I liked to jumped out of my hide—and that was just the beginning! About half the ceiling came crashin' down, takin' 20 feet of stovepipe with it. The soot and plaster dust was so thick you could cut it with a knife. As soon as I heard ol' Raintree chargin' around upstairs, I knew it was time to depart. Only I stopped for a quick look at the hole in the ceiling and that's when I found out the marshal had another shotgun. I saw the muzzle come pokin' down between the joists and I heard the blast a split-second after I dived out the front door. Whew, it was a near thing!

After about five minutes the fire bell rang and I knew I'd better hole up quick or the marshal and his bullyboys would have my hide for certain. I circled around Van Sant's boatyard and followed Crooked Creek until it brought me up behind the sawmill. I finally found the path and I was just gettin' my bearings when I ran smack into a human body comin' the other way. I tell you, that's hard on a man's nerves. I jumped back and tried to run and the other fellow tried to do the same and we both ended up in a heap, clawin' and kickin'.

Then I heard a high-pitched voice callin' for mercy and I knew it was only Cletus Boggs, whose pa runs the livery stable. He's a little younger'n me and about as dumb as they come. It took him three years to get through the third grade and the only reason Professor Howe promoted him was because he got too big for the desks.

When his teeth stopped chatterin', I explained as best I could about the trouble I was in. Right off he treated me like a big hero and when he started beggin' to help, I figured I'd do him a favor and let him. As soon as we got our plans made, he high-tailed it for home, swearin' on his sacred honor and that of his brother and father and Great Uncle Mert he wouldn't give me away. I'm glad he didn't add any more kinfolk, because there ain't a nickel's worth of honor among those last three.

If you were lookin' for a comfortable spot to spend the night, you probably wouldn't pick a 30-foot pile of sawdust, but it makes a middlin' fine hidin' place. Using a stick to cover my tracks, I climbed up a ways and burrowed in, feet first. First I thought I was going to suffocate; then it was so cold and clammy I was afraid I was going to freeze to death. Besides that, the stuff had a sour smell that made me half sick. After about an hour, the sawdust started workin' around inside my clothes and the more I squirmed, the more it itched. I had a couple of cuss words picked out that I'd never used before and I was ready to let 'em go when I saw two lanterns bobbin' up the road. Right then that sawdust pile got mighty cozy. There was three men and the one without a light kept fallin' over things. They poked around the sawmill for a spell and once they stopped right underneath me. All I could think of was what would happed if I'd sneeze. But I didn't and they didn't linger long; in fact, if I had any more visitors, I was sleepin' too hard to know it.

Towards morning I crawled out of my hole and spent a good half hour tryin' to get shut of all my sawdust. With all that molasses underneath, it was like havin' a fur coat. Then I went down on the dock to watch the eastern sky and wait for Cletus. I guess maybe I've been colder in my life, but I can't remember when. All I could think of was a warm fire and a big platter of eggs and fried potatoes. First light was beginning to push up from behind the Illinois bluffs when I heard somebody singin' in between pulls on a set of squeaky oars. There was good ol' Cletus yodelin' along in his brother's jonboat, just like he had good sense.

I was ready to throttle him with my bare hands until he gave me a puppy-dog grin and pulled a bag of food out of his shirt. I never knew cold fried mush and half a loaf of moldy bread could be so tasty. In between bites, I told him to put mud on those noisy oarlocks and I threatened him with an early death if he tried makin' any more music. As soon as it lightened up some, we pushed off for the Illinois shore, gropin' our way through the fog. I figured if I could make it over to Rapids City, I'd be safe from the marshal and then I could worry about findin' the *Jessie Bill*. But after about an hour, all I was interested in was findin' land. Cletus' boat had a strong prejudice against traveling in a straight line; every time I stopped for floatin' ice or to count my blisters, I knew the current was takin' us a little further off course. The fog finally lifted, however, and we bumped ashore a good half-mile below the town. Cletus wouldn't take any money for the trip, and since I didn't have any, I didn't insist. But I gave him my new rabbit's foot and promised him a ride on the *Jessie Bill*.

If it wasn't for Taylor Williams' coalyard, I suppose Rapids City would have disappeared years ago. The mine is located up in the hills a mile and a half away, but Williams built a track and figured out a way to bring those pint-sized cars down to the river by lettin' gravity do all the work. That was back in '71 and I reckon he's made a pile of money sellin' coal to all the packets and those rafters that can afford to burn it.

Most of the stuff is dumped into barges and towed over to LeClaire by the company's little steamer, the *Mary Gilchrist*. You can buy it for eight cents a bushel on the Illinois side or $2.00 a ton at the LeClaire landing. Things was uncommonly quiet when I reached the coalyard and I soon found out that the *Mary Gilchrist* was laid up with a leaky boiler. Two fellows were jawin' at each other outside the office and the one with a high stiff collar and a derby hat let off cussin' long enough to say there wouldn't be any barges movin' until they got a relief boat up from Rock Island. About 9 o'clock I saw a puff of black smoke off to the south and I knew without a second look it was the *Phil Sheridan* standin' upriver on her run to St. Paul. The *Sheridan* is a Northern Line packet and she and the *Milwaukee* put in at LeClaire twice a week—one goin' up and the other downbound for St. Louis. Tomorrow it'll be the *Canada* and the *Sucker State* makin' the same runs.

Mostly, rafters and packets hate each other like poison. If the truth was known, I suppose most raftin' men are jealous of those who work the packets. They're a snooty lot, I can tell you, always actin' like they own the river; yes'n the banks, too. The packets are bigger and faster and there's not a one of them that would give a raft boat the time of day. I asked ol' Pot Belly about it one time and he just snorted. "All that gilt and gingerbread and them fancy uniforms don't mean a damn thing," he said. "Why haulin' passengers and mail don't take no brains. This country could get along without packets a sight faster'n it could raft boats, an' don't you forget it. Who'd brings the lumber down from the north? What would we use to build houses with? And schools and churches? I'm askin' you, who? Why if it wasn't for the rafters, there'd be nobody here but savages!"

I tried to shut him off, but I couldn't. "And let me tell you another thing," he said, gettin' his second wind. "There ain't one packet pilot in fifty who could last five minutes on a rafter. Let him try runnin' Hammond Chute in a crosswind with four acres of logs out in front an' he'll be talkin' to hisself before he's made the first crossing." He went on like that for another five minutes and by the time he'd run down I was plumb sorry I ever asked.

I guess you could say a rafter is built for work while a packet is built for looks and speed. Even the biggest rafters aren't much longer than 165 feet with a narrow beam and a draft that will let you run at low stage. Upper Mississippi packets, on the other hand, may run up to 250 feet in length with beams of 60 or 70 feet. Lower river boats, 'specially those built for the cotton trade, are a heap bigger but you won't find any above St. Louis.

For you landsmen who maybe never seen a raft boat, you take a flat bottom with a rounded stem and a squared-off stern and you call that the boat deck, or the main deck, if you like. The whole place is cluttered up with machinery, startin' with the capstan on the forecastle and workin' back past the boilers and fireboxes. Next comes the open deckhouse with firewood stacked forward and the steam nigger about in the middle. If there's any cargo aboard, it'll be aft of the steam nigger. Back at the stern there's the engine room with a feed pump and two big pitmans that drive the paddlewheel.

Then you put a top over all that and you call it the boiler deck, or sometimes the cabin deck. I know you're going to ask right off why they call it the boiler deck when the boilers are down on the boat deck, but don't expect me to give you a sensible answer. I guess it's because the boilers are located right under the boiler deck and when they blow, it's the boiler deck and everything above it that goes flyin' off to Kingdom Come.

The boiler deck starts right back of the chimneys, comin' up from below. There's one big cabin across the front that's the clerk's office and a loafin' place for those who are off duty. It's got a desk on one side and a bunk where I sleep on the other. Aft of the office is a passageway that runs down the center with cabins on each side. The captain and the pilot always take the best rooms and the other members of the cabin crew fight over what's left.

There's another big cabin at the end of the passageway with the galley on one side and the kitchen on the other. Outside the back door is an open deck above the wheel where you can sleep when it's too hot to breathe in your bunk. The cook's water tank and coal box sit up against the galley wall and there's an open stairway going down to the engine room. Now add another roof, mount the pilothouse on top and you've got yourself a rafter. The rousters and those that aren't part of the cabin crew have to shift for themselves. Mostly they bed down in the deckhouse but those that like a little privacy rig themselves a shelter out on the raft when we're headed downstream.

A packet like the *Sheridan* has also got a boat deck with the usual machinery and a lot more cargo space. Only instead of havin' a sternwheel, it's got two sidewheels located a little aft of the middle of the boat. The buckets are covered with big half-moon boxes, each one painted up with a lot of gaudy pictures. There's a grand stairway with lots of fancy wood that leads from the forecastle to the boiler deck, where the first-class passengers hang out. The staterooms are grouped around the outside edge of the deck with a big salon in the middle. I din't know why they call 'em staterooms because most of 'em are about the size of a rabbit hutch. Some of the fanciest packets have a men's salon and a ladies' salon both. The men's salon has a bar and card tables and no self-respectin' female would be seen there. Foldin' tables are set up in the ladies salon and that's where all the payin' guests gather for chow. The hurricane deck forms the roof of the boiler deck and next comes the texas deck with the pilothouse on top of that. The cabin crew lives on the texas and sometimes there's a plush stateroom up there for the owner and his rich friends. That's what I call livin' high on the hog.

After about 15 minutes at the LeClaire landing, the *Sheridan* cast off and headed straight for Rapids City to fuel up. As I watched her come, I had to admit she was a thing of beauty. Black smoke billowed from her tall stacks and the throb of her engines sounded like a muffled drum. At midstream she whistled, two long blasts and three short ones that sent shivers up my back. Swingin' in from downstream, she slowed on both wheels and I could see General Sheridan painted up there on the starboard paddlebox bigger'n life, spurrin' his big black stallion to the Battle of Winchester. Then the stageplank swung out over the water with a deckhand crouched on the end holding a mooring line in his hand. She was coming fast and anybody who didn't know better would have sworn she was gonna climb the bank. But just at the last minute her engine bell clanged and her wheels churned backwards and stopped, leavin' just enough headway for her bow to nuzzle up to the shore. I don't think I ever seen a prettier landing.

That deckhand was makin' her fast before the plank hit and about 10 more rousters swarmed off behind him, all headin' for the nearest coal barge with their baskets. A red-faced mate prodded 'em along and you could tell he was plenty hot about havin' to make an extra stop for coal. He never said much, but he kept those rousters on the jump. Every once in a while he'd look up at the passengers linin' the rail and scowl, I suppose because he wanted to cuss and couldn't with an audience like that.

Boarding the *Sheridan* never entered my head until I spotted Cash Miller leanin' against the steam capstan. Cash used to pal around with my brother, Luke, and he slept at our place quite a bit until Ma put a stop to it because of his smelly feet. I gave him a hail and he came ashore, takin' care not to get in the way of the rousters and their coal baskets. Quick as I could, I told him my sad story and he had a fallin' down fit when I came to the part about blowin' a hole in the marshal's ceiling. "Ol' Cash'll take care of you," he said and the first thing I knew he was hustlin' me up the plank. You'd of thought he was the master instead of the watchman, but I wasn't in no mood to argue.

"What do they do with stowaways?" I asked when we got out of sight behind a stack of flour barrels.

"You ain't no stowaway," he snapped. "You're a deck passenger that got on before dawn at Muscatine. Hear? All you gotta do is lay low and when we come across the *Jessie Bill* we'll drop you at the next landing." He showed up a little later with a piece of cheese and a cup of coffee and that's the last I saw of him.

I was a little uneasy at first, but nobody paid me any mind and I decided if I was supposed to be a deck passenger my best course was to act like one. There were 25 or 30 of them lollin' around, mostly loggers headin' for the pineries up on the Black and the St. Croix. Let me tell you they were a rough-lookin' lot; some was asleep and some was too full of forty-rod whisky to stand up.

Then there was a bunch of sodbusters jawin' away at whatever it is that farmers talk about and a sickly-lookin' man and his woman with a passel of kids bound for the Dakota country. They were livin' in a high-wheeled freight wagon with a plow lashed to the starboard side and two mules and a cow tied to the back axle. One little shaver told me they'd come all the way from Morgantown, Kentucky, on the Green River and he was mighty put out because he hadn't seen a single Indian on the whole trip. He had a pretty sister about 15 or 16 and for a while I had my hands full tryin' to answer her questions and the kid's, too. But then their ma started nursin' the baby and I cleared out. If there's anything I can't stand, it's a woman nursin' her young'n right out in public.

Every so often I see a write-up in the *Rock Island Argus* tellin' about all the new upper river packets and how the passengers live in style, but they never say anything about the poor critters who ride the boat deck. Bein' a deck passenger is about as low as you can get. There's no seats and no bunks. If you can find a spot that's not taken up with cargo or mail, that's where you ride— until some roustabout tells you you're in the road and runs you off. The only time deck passengers are allowed on the boiler deck is for meals. As soon as the first-class people are fed, they go to their cabins or take a stroll on the hurricane deck while the deck folks and the crew come up to the salon for leftovers.

Cash Miller had told me not to leave the boat deck, but I didn't think he meant for me to starve to death, so when the dinner gong rang, I lined up quick-like with all the others. Everything would have been fine, if it hadn't been for those blasted pink tickets. How was I suppposed to know that every deck passenger had to turn in a little pink ticket every time he got fed? I was halfway through the serving line before I figured out what was going on, so there was nothin' to do but try and bluff it. I told the cook's helper at the end of the line that I lost my ticket and he didn't say anything, so I sat down and started shovelin' it in, thinkin' it might be a short meal.

It was mighty short. Right off the purser tapped me on the shoulder and demanded a ticket. Knowin' it ain't polite to talk with food in your mouth, I kept right on eatin'. That riled him good, because he grabbed me by the collar and jerked me to my feet, pullin' over my chair and causin' a terrible scene. The way he cussed, I figured he used to be a mate. Then with no warning at all, he rapped me across the face with the back of his hand. He shouldn't have done that, because I had a big mouthful of beans and I blew the whole mess all over him. By then I was ready to fight even if he was bigger'n me, but he twisted my arm behind my back and marched me out to the port stairway. About halfway down he gave me a shove and I fell the rest of the way, bangin' my head on the deck. That critter was just plain mean. He drug me over to the fireboxes and pushed me right into the arms of a big sweaty fireman. The fireman never said a word. He handed me a shovel, pointed to the coal pile and right off I knew what he had in mind.

After stokin' a boiler for two hours, my head was throbbin' and my back felt like I'd been kicked by a mule. I kept watchin' the Illinois shore and along late in the afternoon I spotted what I thought was the *Jessie Bill* up at the head of Dutchman's Slough. The fireman was no place in sight, so I ducked out on the guard for a better look. It was the *Jessie Bill* all right, and I don't think she ever looked so good. The only trouble was she was hung up on a shelf of ice, leanin' to port with her wheel clean out of the water. Nobody but ol' *Jessie* could get in a fix like that! For a minute, I couldn't figure it out. Then it came to me that she must've answered a hail from some farmer who had produce to ship and was lookin' for a boat dumb enough to try buckin' through the ice. Packets don't like those out-of-the-way stops and most rafters are in too big a hurry to take on freight on their upstream runs, but there are a few captains like Lafe Clapsaddle who'll pull something crazy when they smell a few greenbacks. Most of the ice in the slough was rotten and you could see where the *Jessie Bill* had gone through without much trouble until she pushed up in the neck like a rat headin' straight into a trap.

Right about then I turned around and there was that bug-eyed fireman comin' at me like a crazy man. I saw his shovel out of the corner of my eye and I ducked, only it wasn't quite quick enough. The next thing I knew I was layin' up against a stanchion and the whole boat was goin' around in circles, slow and lazy like. I could feel the blood oozin' along my ear and for the next hour or so I didn't much care whether I lived or died. I reckon if I hadn't looked around, that fool fireman would have parted my skull clean down to my adam's apple. When the boat whistled for a landing, I roused up some and found me a nice piece of two-by-four in case ol' Sweaty showed up again. He did, too, but this time he just laughed and said he was going to put me ashore as soon as we tied up at Savanna.

He followed me to the forecastle and when I tried to make a run for it, he caught my arm and jerked me back. "Not so fast, kid," he sneered. "That stageplank's for payin' guests only." Then he gave a big lunge and I went head-over-teacup into ten feet of ice water. It wasn't much consolation, but I got a death grip on his shirt as I fell and we hit together in one big splash.

While he was bellowin' for help and gaspin' for breath, I lit out for shore as fast as I could swim. It wasn't far, but another foot or so and I never would've made it. I just laid there, too cold to move. I guess I would have died right there on the bank, except I heard those roustabouts laughin' fit to kill, and that got my dander up.

I was cussin' and bawlin' and throwin' mud all at the same time. I don't know if I hit anybody, but I sure enough took the shine off Phil Sheridan's spankin' blue uniform.

Chapter Four

*It was night and ahead of us
the Mississippi River and the Illinois
bluffs had disappeared. We were
heading up into a black wall. Now
it was up to Mr. Pilot.*
—Richard Bissell

APRIL 19, 1880:

Nothin' says you have to be crazy to be a good raft pilot, but it must help some. I don't know of one worth his salt who ain't touched in the head in one way or another. What I haven't figured out is whether they was a little daft to begin with or got that way fightin' logs down 700 miles of river.

There's a heap of famous pilots on the upper river, like Sandy McPhail with his red beard, ol' Charlie LaPointe, Sam Van Sant and Frenchman Joe Guardapie, who can cuss in four languages. And that's hardly a start. There's J. B. McCoy, who they say can lick any four men in his crew, and those don't-give-a-damn Buisson brothers—Joe, Henry and Cy. And I don't want to forget Abe Lincoln's cousin, Stephen Hanks. They tell me he is one of the few honest men in Albany, Illinois, and a real God-fearin' gentleman.

Every raftsman spends a good share of the winter hunkered around a stove somewhere arguin' about who's the best pilot on the river. For my money, nobody can hold a candle to Wabasha

Dan Wilson. I've heard more'n one river rat say that in his prime, he was the top pilot between St. Anthony's Falls and the Head of the Passes. And not just piloting rafters, you understand, but cotton boats, packets, coal boats—anything that floats.

The only trouble is Dan has some other claims to fame, too, such as havin' a disposition like a sackful of rattlesnakes and bein' able to drink enough forty-rod whisky to float a keelboat. I suppose if it wasn't for his boozin', he'd still be senior pilot on the *Grand Republic*. He drifted from one boat to another until he finally hit bottom and had to make a choice between goin' thirsty and workin' on the *Jessie Bill*. Cap'n Lafe snorts around and threatens to fire him every time he goes on a bender, but nobody pays him any mind—least of all Wabasha Dan. I reckon we could get along without our rudders sooner'n we could without Dan, and nobody knows it better'n foxy ol' Lafe.

When you first see him at a distance, Dan reminds you of a banty rooster or maybe a feisty little terrier. But up close you see that long nose and those gray eyes and it's more like bein' face to face with a killer hawk. For a little man, he leaves a mighty big wake. He stands only about five-foot-two and I don't suppose he'd weigh more'n 130 pounds with a couple of lead lines stuffed in his pockets. His eyes hardly blink and his mouth never smiles, or if it does you can't see it under that walrus mustache of his. Four-Mile Freeman saw him whip a steamboatman once who outweighed him by a hundred pounds. "I'd sooner tangle with a buzz saw," Four-Mile said. "He's quicker'n a cat and he carries a knife in the top of his boot that can part a man from his gizzard in only two swipes."

It's an unwritten law on the river that when a pilot takes the wheel, he's king. He has all the say when it comes to navigation and not even the captain can overrule him. Only with Wabasha Dan, it's like he's an Oriental potentate and Lafe Clapsaddle and all the rest of us are members of his harem. You wouldn't believe the way he abuses the captain. He only speaks to him once or twice a week; mostly he gives him a cold-eyed stare that sends Lafe off lookin' for his wine jug.

It's also a genuine honor to be allowed inside Dan's pilot-house. Most of the time there are at least four or five hands on this ol' tub who wouldn't dare step across the threshold when he's at the helm. The exact number varies from day to day, according to the mood Dan's in. One person who'll never see the inside of the pilothouse, sure, is Bush McDonald. Thanks to him, I'm stuck with all the cleanin' up there. He's the watchman and he's supposed to take care of jobs like that. His name is really Bushnell, only we all call him Bushel-Butt because that best describes the size and shape of his rear end. It all started over the pilothouse cuspidor. Bush hated to clean it and he'd never do it until Dan made him. Then he figured out a way to do it without gettin' his hands dirty—just tie a line on it and drag it behind the boat for a while. But one day the line slipped and the cuspidor ended up on the bottom of the river. The thing came from Constantinople and it was solid brass. "Killing would be too good for that nincompoop kid," I heard Dan tell the captain.

That's when I took over the cleanin'. Dan is fussy and he wants the side windows washed every day and the floor scrubbed once, maybe twice a week. At first I was plenty mad, but I've decided it's not so bad after all. Cleve is Dan's steersman and I like listenin' to all the things Dan tells him about runnin' the river. Dan never lets on, but I can tell he likes Cleve and he's willing to learn him a few things as long as Cleve don't push him. Usually, it takes two to three years to get a pilot's license. The way it works, you sign up with some pilot who's willing to take you as a cub. As soon as you know enough to run the boat, he sits on the lazy bench and you do all the work. This costs money, mind you. As soon as you get your license and land a job, then you have to pay.

But Wabasha Dan doesn't want cubs and he doesn't want their money. He'll do it all for free if he thinks you've got the makings of a pilot. I think Cleve already knows more'n most pilots. He was steersman on the *Alhambra* for a year or so and he's willin' to put up with the *Jessie Bill* as long as Dan is the pilot. Cleve's got his own system of rating pilots. He calls Dan a crackerjack and that's the top. Then he laughs and calls Captain Lafe a bridge-buster and that's the bottom.

Let me tell you, it's a real show watchin' Dan put a six-brail raft through the Rock Island bridge in the fog or sneak over

Chimney Rock bar when there's hardly enough water to wet your feet. Pure art, Cleve calls it. When Cleve's got the wheel, he and Dan don't pay any attention to me and I learn a little just be keepin' my ears open. Dan calls 'em the principles of piloting. Just the other day, he was goin' on about two boats runnin' side by side. When they do that, the river will draw them together, I mean up close. Say one of the boats had less power than the other. All she has to do is hold against the other boat, and the one with the most power can't get past her. I guess if you was in a race, you'd need to know that. And I learned another thing. Say your boat is in shallow water and you're prayin' for another foot or two. The boat will sheer off to the deeper water if there's any close, and you don't have to do a thing. Think of that.

Dan's got a mean streak in him and a hot temper to go with it. Pa used to say he'd charge hell with nothin' but a bucket of water and never bat an eye. If you was to make a list of Dan's pet hates, you'd have to put calliope players, preachers, cats and the Women's Christian Temperance Union up near the top. One time when he was pilot on the *City of Louisville* on the Ohio, he grabbed the calliope player off his bench and pitched him over the side because he didn't like the way he played "Buffalo Gal."

After Rutherford B. Hayes won the election of '76, Dan allowed he was going to be the greatest man since Washington. But after he read where Mrs. Hayes was called "Lemonade Lucy" because she wouldn't permit any booze in the White House, he's been cussin' the president ever since. Yes, and the Cabinet and Congress and the Supreme Court, too.

You'd think Dan would hate the *Jessie Bill* most of all. He don't, though. Oh, he bad-mouths her and he's always tellin' somebody what a bad handler she is. But mostly he just tolerates her, like you would your old grandma, who's stoved up and lost her teeth and don't have anybody to look after her proper. Sometimes he'll even give her a little sweet talk when he's at the helm and thinks no one can hear him. And it must pay off, because he can do things with her you'd think would be nigh on to impossible. I guess maybe it's because he understands her.

I only got in trouble with Dan once and you can bet it won't happen again. I was washin' windows and mindin' my own business when he blasted me. "No whistling in this pilothouse!" he shouted, and I almost jumped out of my skin. Especially, since I didn't even know I'd been whistling.

"Don't you know it's bad luck to whistle in the pilothouse?"

"No, sir."

"Well, you know it now and I don't want it to happen again. Is that clear?"

"YES, SIR!" I said it with great feeling.

Wabasha Dan's got one more hate I almost forgot about: the river. So help me, that's the truth. To hear him tell it, bein' a steamboatman is in the same class as rustlin' cattle or robbin' graves. I can't figure him out, because you'd have to hog-tie him to keep him off the river. But that's the way he is. He's got a funny way of talkin', too, and if you interrupt him, he'll take your head clean off. He sort of spits out his words in little chopped-up bunches. Then he'll quit right in the middle of what he's sayin' and it may be 10 minutes or so before he starts in again.

"Take my advice, young'un, and don't let the river get in your blood," he told me once. "You're a ring-tailed fool if you do."

I didn't say nothin' and pretty soon he goes back at it. "A dirty, schemin' ol' bitch, that's what she is." I didn't know what he was talkin' about, but I didn't dare ask. Then he gave the engine room a slow bell and we sneaked around a sandbar that was workin' its way out from the Illinois shore. About a half hour went by and the only sound was when he whistled for an upstream packet. I was dozin' some on account of I hadn't had much sleep the night before and I jumped when he broke the silence.

"Every river is a bitch and the Mississippi is the biggest of the lot. Them that call it the Father of Waters don't know what they're talkin' about. Anything as treacherous as this river has got to be female. The minute you start trustin' her and think you got her eatin' out of your hand, she'll turn on you every time. When she's smilin' at you and you got a straight stretch of water with no bottom, that's when you want to look out. There's nothing that makes a river as happy as bustin' up steamboats. She's got snags and bars and sawyers and deadheads and a hundred other things in her bag of tricks. No end to 'em. Besides that, she gets an awful lot of help from all the chuckleheaded rubes who think they know how to run her.

"If you want to be a pilot, boy, you got to hate her and fight her every mile of the way. And you can tell 'em ol' Wabasha Dan said so."

Right then it came to me why Dan is a drinkin' man. I reckon when you're hatin' and fightin' a river all the time, it takes a lot of forty-rod to keep you primed and on your toes.

Cleve Allen says Dan operates on about a pint of whisky a day, more or less. You'd think that would hold any raftsman, but every couple of months he gets extra dry and then you may not see hide nor hair of him for three days. He never causes any trouble; he just lays on his bunk and pours it down 'til he can't hold any more. After that he sleeps it off and when you go past his cabin door, you can hear him snorin' away. Then he puts down a quart or two of Fatback's coffee and tells Cap'n Clapsaddle to get the hell out of his pilothouse.

A good steamboatman could spot Wabasha Dan anywhere on the face of the earth and know right off he's a river pilot. I guess it's the proud way he walks and the way he squints his eyes, sizin' up a mile of river without turnin' his head, all the time measuring all the little signs that tell him where the best water is and how much bottom he's got.

Dan's no ladies' man, but he's fussy about his clothes and neat as a pin. He always wears a white shirt with a black string tie and he wouldn't touch the wheel without his black kid gloves. He wears 'em winter and summer and it takes him about five minutes to put 'em on, tuggin' and pullin' until each finger is just right.

Until you see Dan in the pilothouse, you'd figure a little squirt like him wouldn't be no match for a six-foot wheel. But there's where you'd be dead wrong. He's got a box he stands on so he can see over the top and he can make that wheel do everything but talk. First off he reaches up on the shelf and sticks a long cheroot in his mouth. Only he never lights it; he just keeps chewin' away until there's nothin' left. If a man's a sloppy tobacco-chewer, he won't be spending much time in Dan's pilothouse. About every hour he lets fly with a little flip of his chin and he hits the cuspidor everytime. I've never seen him miss yet.

Last summer some crony of the captain's came aboard with about a half-pound of Granger Twist stuck in his jaw. He was perched up on the lazy bench like he owned the boat and he kept eyin' the sandbox where the stove sits in the middle of the pilot-house. Pretty soon he unloaded in that general direction and Dan whirled around and read him the riot act before the poor ol' codger could wipe his chin. The abuse was more'n he could stand and he eased out the door and kind of slunk down the ladder like a whipped dog.

When we're in bad water or cuttin' a tight bend, Dan navigates with his feet as well as his hands. That's right. He climbs that wheel like a monkey until he gets it where he wants it; then he drops off and lets it spin free until just the right moment when he brings it up short again. Like as not, he don't even watch the head of the raft because he knows just where it's going to be. It's a sight to behold.

But here I am off course again, 'cause I haven't told you a thing about what happened to me after I got throwed off the *Phil Sheridan*. Maybe that wasn't the blackest day of my life, but it didn't miss it much. I stumbled off down the road wondering what kind of luck it took for a body to be wet, cold, hungry, beat and bruised all at the same time. I didn't even know where I was goin', but I kept movin' downriver, hopin' the road would take me somewhere close to Dutchman's Slough. I figured it must be about 15 miles, but the way it turned out it was closer to 20. I rode a piece with some loose-jawed farmer, but he asked so many questions about what I was doin' and where I was goin' that I was glad when he turned inland.

Along late in the afternoon I knew I couldn't cut it much farther, so I sneaked into the next barn I come to and burrowed me a nest in a big pile of hay. I don't know how I could sleep when I was shakin' all over from the cold, but that's what I must have been doin' when I heard a dog barkin' like crazy and felt somebody stirrin' up my bed like he meant business. A pitchfork in my backside was about the last thing I needed, so I came out with my hands up, lookin' as peaceable as I could. There stood a little fat farmer and the first thing he did was run out of the barn and yell bloody-murder for his wife. She got there in about two shakes with a shotgun and they marched me up to the house like I was Jesse James hisself.

I guess maybe I bawled a little when I got in where it was warm and that turned out to be the only smart thing I'd done all day. I gave 'em some cock and bull story about runnin' away from my cruel step-father and the next thing I knew they had me decked out in some dry clothes and were fillin' me up with hot corn bread and honey. After that I had trouble stayin' awake and when they got their chores done they fixed me a bed beside the kitchen stove. I wanted to hang around and thank 'em in the worst way, but I woke up before daylight and I decided I'd better hike before they figured out all those tales I'd been tellin' didn't hang together very well.

First I thought it was the weather that had me sweatin' and freezin' all at the same time. Then I started feelin' worse by the minute and I knew I was ailin' bad. My bones ached from the inside out and the only time I smiled all morning was when I got to thinkin' about Wabasha Dan and how mad he must be about gettin' beached on the ice. Cleve said he was just like a wet settin' hen, but I wasn't around to watch him perform. In fact, if it wasn't for Cleve, I maybe wouldn't be around at all. To tell the truth, I don't even remember gettin' to Dutchman's Slough. When Cleve saw me staggerin' around on the bank, he hustled me across the ice to the *Jessie Bill* and put me to bed in his bunk. And right there I stayed for the near part of a week, fightin' a roarin' fever and missin' out on all the fun. I don't know which was worse—the fever or Cleve's doctoring. If a mustard poultice and five pounds of goose grease don't kill you first, it's bound to make you well.

It took three days and a chunk of Captain Lafe's cash to get us out of the ice. Everybody knows that Wabasha Dan is too smart to get caught in a trap like that, but when the captain is dead set on makin' a fool of hisself, Dan is always ready to oblige him. First Lafe had everybody out on the ice tryin' to chop us free. Then he had the bright idea he could build a bunch of fires and melt his way out, but he gave that up in a hurry when the wind sprung up and came near to settin' the boat afire. Finally he throwed up his hands and sent Freeman and a couple of others out in the yawl to hail another boat and get some help. The first boat to pass was the *Frontenac*, a Fort Madison rafter, and she wouldn't give us the time of day. The next one was the *R. J. Wheeler* out of Muscatine. Her captain, Mike Oliver, laughed his head off and said he'd be back around the Fourth of July after the ice had a chance to soften up.

Freeman started throwin' his weight around about that time and the third boat—she was the *Eclipse* from Rock Island— headed up the slough to look things over. Black Jack Davis owned the boat and having had a few too many dealings with our captain, he demanded $50, cash in advance, before he'd turn a hand. I guess ol' Lafe hollered like a stuck hog, but Black Jack had him over a barrel and he knew it. So he paid, but he got it back on Davis a little by makin' him wait while we took on the cargo we'd come after in the first place. And do you know what it was? Six crates of scruffy-lookin' chickens consigned to a produce house in Dubuque. If those fowls laid golden eggs they still couldn't have paid what it cost to haul 'em. Pot Belly got steam up while the rousters chopped enough ice to free the paddle buckets. Then the *Eclipse* came about and eased in on a reverse bell, puttin' the two boats stern to stern. Four-Mile and Black Jack had a few words about the best way to secure the lines, but they finally struck a compromise and 30 minutes later we were in the clear and out in the channel.

Bein' sick abed is bad enough, but when a body gets back on his feet, all shaky and weak, and finds out he's been sacked, well that's just about the last straw. Cleve tried to tell me what had happened, only he was so mad he couldn't get the words out. But Bush McDonald, he was blabbin' all over the boat. "Been promoted to clerk," he says right off, grinnin' like a cat in a bucket of cream, "and you're now the cook's helper and watchman. What ya think of that?" I wanted to punch his fat, ugly face only I didn't have an ounce of strength to spare.

Now everybody in LeClaire'll tell you Bush is a big slob of a kid who ain't good for anything except rubbin' folks the wrong way. Some people in this world are thick-skulled and some are lazy, but Bush is both. Honest, he wouldn't know how to pour you-know-what out of a boot if the directions was printed on the heel. Let me tell you, I had my Irish up. I hot-footed it up the ladder and beat on the captain's door so hard it hurt my knuckles. He must've thought it was Wabasha Dan, because he opened the shutters slow like without sayin' a word. Then when he saw it was me, he took off on a big harangue about how he ought to dock my pay for missin' the boat and not bein' able to stand watch after I got back.

You talk about gratitude! After what I'd been through, most captains would've given me an extra week's pay, or maybe a medal or something. Pretty soon he slacked off a little and I put it to him straight: "Do I get my old job back or do I quit?" Those were my exact words.

Then he says "You won't do neither, boy. You're fired!"

Since the discussion wasn't gettin' anywhere, I just turned around and left him standin' there. My temper has a way of slippin' out from under me when I need it most, and I began to see maybe I had trapped myself with that last question. I knew he wouldn't stop the boat until we had to make a landing for wood or supplies and I figured I could put up with anything for a day or two. But a man's got his pride and movin' my gear out of the clerk's office down to the boat deck wasn't easy, I'll tell you.

Just watchin' Bush operate was enough to turn your stomach. He had sense enough to stay out of the pilothouse, but he was everywhere else, stickin' his nose in where it didn't belong and just makin' an ass out of hisself in general. It go so bad that I finally spoke a little prayer, askin' the Lord if He could see His way to cuttin' Bush down a notch or two before he got clean out of hand. My Ma used to say that prayer is the finest thing in the world, only you shouldn't expect the Lord to do things just the way you want Him to.

Well, this time Ma was wrong, because I got results all right and it didn't take more'n three or four hours. I was luggin' stove wood for ol' Fatback when I heard a terrible racket in the galley. Bush came bustin' out the door with Fatback hot on his heels, swingin' a cleaver and yellin' like a wild man.

Fatback is the only livin' cadaver I've ever met. He's all skin and bones with a hump back and a face that would look a lot better on a horse. Most of his teeth are gone and he's got a handlebar mustache that catches fire once in a while when he gets down too close to the stove. Judgin' from the way he smells up close, I'd say he takes a bath maybe every spring. And you ought to see the buckskin pants he wears; they're so stiff with dirt and grease he likely has trouble makin' 'em bend at the knees. He won the title of the worst cook on the river back before the war and nobody has ever been able to take it away from him. I never heard his real name and for all I know, he doesn't have one. But Fatback fits him, because it's about all he ever serves; that and sowbelly and fried mush. I swear he knows 15 ways to cook a piece of fatback—all of 'em bad.

When it comes to flyin' off the handle, Fatback is second only to Wabasha Dan. Like I told you, he can't see much past the end of his nose and I guess that's why he gets so het up when you snitch food out of the galley. This time he had blood in his eye and I knew if he ever let fly with that cleaver, Bush was a goner. Both of them went pilin' down the ladder and along the port guard. Somewhere along the way Bush must have grabbed a pike pole for protection; leastwise he had one in his hand when he went through the deckhouse and came out on the starboard side.

According to Four-Mile, Fatback was gainin' as they reached the front end. Bush was tryin' to look back over his shoulder and just as he got to the stack of chicken crates, his pole hooked one of the slats. You can guess what happened! The whole shebang went over with a crash and you never saw such a mess of kindlin' wood and chicken feathers in your whole life. What a racket those chickens made! There must have been close to 200 of them and they went off in all directions, flyin' and flappin'. I thought I'd split, sure.

Within three minutes those scrawny birds were all over the boat, including two rows of them roosting on the spreader bars between the chimneys. Two of them got in the pilothouse before Wabasha Dan could shut the door and I thought we was gonna climb the bank before he caught 'em and wrung their necks.

The captain was in a neck-wringin' mood, too, only he was huntin' Bush and not birds. He found him hidin' down in the hold and right then and there is when I got my job back—thanks to the Good Lord and those Dutchman's Slough chickens.

Chapter Five

*Up and down the river the glinting
saws flashed, sawdust piles
grew larger, and still the logs came.
The rafts continued to grow in size
until it seemed that it would be
humanly impossible to guide them
down the river.*
—Marquis Childs

APRIL 28, 1880:

One thing's certain—there ain't another place on the Mississippi the likes of Beef Slough. Bar none, it's the biggest rafting works in the world. Oh, there's other places like Lake St. Croix up by Stillwater, and West Newton, below Belvedire Island, but they don't hold a candle to Beef Slough.

You could say Beef Slough is sort of a branch mouth of the Chippewa River. It leaves the main channel at Round Hill and meanders down along the Wisconsin Bluffs for about 12 miles before it opens into the Mississippi above Alma. There's more goin' on in those 12 miles than any spot above St. Louis. The whole thing is run by the Mississippi River Logging Company and they got the job of makin' rafts down pretty fine. As soon as the ice goes out, logs come pouring down the Chippewa by the jillions. From then until freeze-up, the place is spillin' over with wild-eyed lumberjacks and dirty-necked raftsmen.

Floatin' the winter's cut of pine down the Chippewa is one thing, but herdin' all those logs into the right spot and keepin' folks from stealin' 'em after they're there is something else. The big lumber outfits start out by putting their own marks on the log butts when they're cut—like branding cattle out West. Weyerhaeuser and Denkmann use a big X and the Shaw Company has a funny mark that looks like a pollywog. The Hamiltons use a cross with a gable over the top of it.

Logs are mighty contrary when they're comin' down a crooked river on a spring rise and the people who run the sheer-booms have to know their stuff. In case you never seen one, a sheer-boom is made out of logs or sometimes 12 by 12 timbers bolted together to make sort of a floating corral about six feet wide and as long as it needs to be.

To begin with, they anchor a big boom over on the right bank of the Chippewa and drape it across the main channel to funnel everything into the head of Beef Slough. The boom is hooked together in 300-foot sections and it stays closed all season. Inside the slough the water's slack and the logs ain't in such a hurry. Everywhere you look there are long rows of pilings that split the place into chutes and pens. Each chute's got its own sheer-boom that swings open with the current. After you draw off a batch of logs, you close the boom with a windlass and start throwin' together a raft. Only it ain't quite as easy as I make it sound. Sometimes the sheer-boom breaks or you take on a string of logs that belong to somebody else and then there's hell to pay while you sort out the whole mess and start over again.

A few of the big lumber outfits operate their own boats and if they all did that the *Jessie Bill* would be out of luck. But most companies are only interested in finding the best market downstream and they'll charter any boat they figure can deliver a raft in one piece. You maybe wonder how an ol' tub like the *Jessie Bill* can get any business at all, but the truth is most of the time there's more rafts waitin' to go downriver than there are rafters to push 'em. A mill owner who won't look at you early in the season may come around on bended knee when he can't find a fast boat and he knows the price of lumber is goin' down every day in Dubuque or Clinton.

Now Cap'n Lafe, he's mighty cagey and not above cuttin' his rates when he finds a small operator who's afraid of the market and maybe needs to save a few dollars here and there. I could tell he was gettin' nervous when we sighted our first raft at McGregor. The *St. Croix* was pushin' it and it was something to behold as it came slidin' through the morning mist hanging along the Iowa bluffs. We whistled for four or five more before we tied up at Alma last Friday and by then I knew ol' Clapsaddle was ready to dicker and deal.

But the way it turned out, the only people he had any dealings with was a one-eyed justice of the peace and some quack doctor. The first night Mudcat Lewis and Limber Jim Gray got throwed in jail for wreckin' the dance hall and it cost the captain three bucks apiece to get 'em out. Then on Saturday night some rouster off the *Kate Keen* tried to carve up Argonaut Smith with a busted bottle and this doctor charged two dollars for sewin' his left ear back on. Lafe was plenty mad about that and he said he wouldn't pay it until the doctor got huffy and allowed he'd quarantine our boat for every disease in the book and one or two that hadn't been written in yet.

Early Sunday morning I heard the captain tell Pot Belly to make steam because we couldn't afford to hang around a crummy place like Alma. I figured we'd head up to Wabasha or Read's Landing over on the Minnesota side, but I didn't see how that would help our chances of finding a raft. The big lumber outfits have men in all three towns and you can't so much as turn a paddle without them knowin' about it. From Alma it's only about a mile to the mouth of Beef Slough and another five will take you on to Wabasha. From there it's a little better'n three miles to Read's Landing at the foot of Lake Pepin. All three are what you'd call jumpin' towns and if the Mississippi and the Chippewa ever went dry all of a sudden, you could find enough whisky in all the saloons to float out most of the logs.

We was ready to cast off our lines when some dapper little fellow came puffin' across the plank wavin' his hat and callin' for the captain. After about 20 minutes the two of them came down from the office and I could tell by the big smile on Lafe's face that we was in business. The captain had a hold of the man's arm and they stood on the front end for five minutes carryin' on like a couple of politicians.

As soon as he was gone, ol' Clapsaddle stuck his thumbs behind his galluses and strutted around like a rooster. "That was Mr. Burdock," he announced, all important like. "He's the head buyer for S. and J. C. Atlee Company of Fort Madison and he knows a good, dependable boat when he sees one."

Something caused Four-Mile to choke on his tobacco, but the captain didn't pay no attention. "As soon as I showed him my credentials," he crowed, "he insisted on the services of this boat. When I told him I'd have to think it over, he offered us $110 a brail with a premium of $50 if we make delivery in six days."

It would be at least three days before they'd have a raft ready for us and ol' Pot Belly said that was a lucky thing because he needed time to reseat that bad starboard piston. "If that blasted thing keeps rockin' like it's been doin', we won't get to Fort Madison by freeze-up," he grumbled.

Pot Belly had some others things to say, too, mainly about Mr. Burdock and what a sucker he was to offer those rates so early in the season. "A'fore Lafe Clapsaddle gets through with him, he'll be lucky to keep his eye teeth." Then Pot Belly gave himself a reverse bell and started his mind off in the opposite direction. He's always doin' that. "Maybe that Burdock ain't as dumb as he looks," he said, puttin' a greasy paw on my next-to-last clean shirt. "Maybe the Atlees got some kind of a scheme goin', one of those sneaky deals to drive up the price of lumber. Let me tell you, them big companies bear watchin', the way they take advantage of the little guy."

The next morning Four-Mile took me up to Beef Slough to see what kind of a raft they were building for us. Any clerk worth his salt, he told me, has got to know how many logs he has and where every last one of 'em is until delivery is made. We went up on the *Lion*, a dinky steam packet that makes two runs a day up through the lower end of the slough, landing at the logging company headquarters to let off mail, freight and passengers. Then she heads out through the cutoff on her way to Wabasha and Read's Landing.

Now Four-Mile couldn't give a hoot whether Atlee or Weyerhaeuser or the Devil hisself owned the logs. All he cared about was a raft that was put together the way he thought it ought to be. "She's got to have just enough give to her so we can bend her some," he said in that bull voice of his. "But by God, she's got to be tight, too, so's she won't make an ape's tail the first time we bump an island or put one corner up on a bar."

The Mississippi River Logging Company headquarters is a big barn of a place stuck up on pilings with a bunch of offices across the front and a mess hall and bunkrooms in the back. They never built it for looks, I'll tell you. Besides catchin' and sortin' everything that hits the slough, the company scales the logs and builds the rafts, complete with check works and guy line pins— all for 75 cents per 1,000 feet. I don't know what they pay, but I wouldn't have one of their jobs for all the gold in Colorado. Those crazy Swedes and Norwegians hop around on those slippery logs like they was at a Saturday night hoedown. When they ain't workin', they're drinkin' and fightin' and cuttin' each other up with canthooks. I wouldn't get within 10 feet of those people if I could help it, but Four-Mile has to be right up on the front row where he can straw-boss the whole job. Mostly, lumberjacks don't take kindly to a riverman tellin' 'em how to build a raft. When you're as big and mean-lookin' as Freeman, however, I guess they're willing to make exceptions.

To build a raft, you start out with a brail 600 feet long and 45 feet wide. Three brails make a half-raft or what some call a piece; when you put two pieces together you got a floating woodpile that's 600 feet long and 270 feet wide.

A good crew can throw together a brail in less than a day's time. First off, they sort out the longest logs and butt up the ends with about a 30-inch lap to make the frame. These are the boom logs and they're fastened together with three links of heavy chain. They bore a nine-inch hole into each log where they lap over and then they drive a green oak pin through the end link of each chain. When three sides of the frame is done, they make it fast to the pilings and let what current there is carry in the loose logs. That's when those fool lumberjacks go into their dance, swingin' their pike poles and peavies and herdin' those logs like they was so many sheep. You understand those logs can't go in any which-way; they have to line up just right and fit snug, end-wise to the current. From then on it's easy: they frame in the open end and rig some half-inch cross wires to keep her from spreadin' and the brail is done.

Early in the afternoon two men showed up in a double-headed skiff and hitched on to our first brail, lettin' it drop down maybe a mile to where they could get it out of the road and snub it to the bank. As soon as the third brail came down, a finishing crew took over and laid them is so all three were even at the stern. They they fastened them together and as soon as they finished buildin' the snubbin' works, we had a half-raft ready to go.

Four-Mile was hopin' we could go up the slough the next morning and bring out the first piece, but ol' Pot Belly whined around and said it would take one more day to doctor up his sick piston. It was noon Wednesday before we got hitched up and I don't think I ever worked so hard in my life. First we put on new crosswires and pulled the whole piece as taut as we could with windlass poles. I won't bother to tell you how a windlass pole works, but it's a man-killin' machine.

Four-Mile was runnin' the whole show, cussin' and shoutin' and givin' orders to everybody including the captain. Wabasha Dan eased the boat around and got her centered on the buttin' block on the first try. Without a buttin' block to tow on, you'd never get a raft past the first bend. It's a whale of a big log chained to the middle of the stern boom and if it ever comes loose, you're in a heap of trouble. To get everything hitched in proper, Four-Mile split us up in pairs and started runnin' lines. You'd never believe how many it takes to hold a boat and several thousand logs together. First there's the head lines that go straight out to the check works so you got something to back on. Then the breast lines are run out to the front corners of the raft to keep the stern of the boat snug on the buttin' block and after that comes the guy lines which tie the stern corners to the steam nigger for steering. After Four-Mile cussed some more and made us take up a little slack here and there, we went at it again with the A lines and the corner lines. By the time we fastened the monkey line from the forward boom to the buttin' block, that half-raft was laced up like a fat woman in her Sunday corset.

I don't like to interrupt my own story, but maybe I'd better tell you what a steam nigger is, just so you don't get too confused.

Most pilots wouldn't touch a raft boat if it didn't have one because it's the only thing goin' that can halfway steer a raft. You start out with two big spools or drums, mounted side by side. Both spools are wrapped with one-and-a-half-inch line, one goin' to the port corner of the raft and one to the starboard corner.

Each spool has a steam pipe which makes it turn, one to the left and one to the right. If you're runnin' the steam nigger, you better remember which is left and which is right. When the pilot rings one bell, you hit the right valve and that pulls the stern of the boat to starboard; if you get two bells you hit the left valve and the stern swings to port.

Four-Mile explained it pretty well when he said what you're doin' is usin' the whole boat like it was one big rudder. Pot Belly goes on about pilots who get a little jumpy when they find themselves in a tight place and they ring too many bells in too big a hurry. "When you're tryin' to run that machine down below and you got a Swiss bell-ringer up above, there's hell to pay," he said.

Movin' a half-raft out of Beef Slough wouldn't be no trick at all if it wasn't for another dozen or so pieces and maybe six or seven boats all gettin' in each other's road. To keep people from killin' each other, the *Little Hoddie* comes in and kind of sorts 'em out one at a time. The *Little Hoddie* is a bow boat operated by the logging company. She's some smaller than a regular rafter and that makes her a good handler in tight places. Pot Belly's piston sounded healthy again as we backed out and the *Hoddie* hitched in sideways across the bow of the raft. Then we started inchin' our way down the slough with the *Hoddie* swinging the head end first to port and then to starboard to get us past the other pieces. Once we reached the closing boom at the foot of the slough, Four-Mile waved off the bow boat and we had the whole river to ourselves. About five o'clock we tied up under a bar a half mile above Alma and most of the crew lit out for town to get shut of what little money they had left.

The next morning Argonaut Smith and me took the yawl to Alma to pick up a fresh batch of sidemeat and some more check line while the rest of the crew unhitched the half-raft and got things ready to go after the second piece. Along about two o'clock Four-Mile hailed the *Lion* and the two of us headed up the slough to check on the rest of our raft and get our bill of lading at headquarters. Black clouds were rollin' up in the west and by the time we got inside the boom, it was rainin' cats and dogs. This didn't help Four-Mile's disposition none, because he was countin' big on picking up the second piece at daylight and gettin' us all tied in and started downriver by the next afternoon. The rain was comin' down hard enough to drown a goose when we got to the company wharfboat and it was plain there'd be no more raft-buildin' that day. I was waitin' for them to drop the plank when Freeman whacked me on the shoulder. "To hell with that raft, boy," he said. "We're goin' on to Wabasha to visit the Queen of Vicksburg!"

"Who's boat is that?" I asked, wonderin' where he got that chessy-cat grin all of a sudden.

"Good Lord a'mighty, where you been all your life?" he roared. "The Queen of Vicksburg ain't no boat! She's a fire-eatin' whisky-drinkin' flesh-an'-blood woman, that's what she is, and there ain't another'n like her on the whole of this river."

Freeman is a hard one to figure. He can blow his stack one minute and then be laughin' the next and I guess there's nothin' wrong with that except he's liable to break your neck in between. Cleve Allen says there's not a stronger or louder mate on the upper river and I got no cause to doubt it. He got his nickname years ago on the *R. J. Wheeler* when some flannel-headed rouster let fly with an ax and cut the starboard guy line. The head of the raft made a big dido toward the bank and lines started poppin' all over the place before they could get stopped. Four-Mile let out a roar that bounced from one bank to the other and then he cussed that deckhand for five solid minutes without repeatin' hisself once.

According to the story, this all happened when the *Wheeler* was near the foot of Big Island below Burlington. The crew of the *Lady Grace* all swore they could hear him cussin' as they passed the mouth of the Skunk River and that's an even four miles downstream. I asked Freeman about it once and he said it was nothin' but a lot of blow made up by Kelly Yates, captain of the *Lady Grace*. "Ol' Yates was a born liar," he said. "If a member of his crew ever forgot and told the truth, Kelly paid him off and put him ashore right on the spot."

By the time we landed at Wabasha, I was worryin' about what I was gettin' into. "Is this Vicksburg woman a close friend of yours?" I asked Four-Mile.

"Friend!" he bellowed. "She's a heap more than that. She's the only true love I ever had. Why, she can do more for a riverman in five minutes than any run-of-the-mill female can do in five years."

"Then why don't you marry her?"

That hit Four-Mile right on the funny bone. "I guess you'd say she's not the marryin' kind. She's got way too much love for just one man. Besides that, she's a businesswoman with a whole covey of little girls to support."

"I thought you said she wasn't married?"

"I did."

"Then how'd she get a bunch of little girls?"

"Damn me, boy, I didn't know you was so dumb. They ain't her own, they just work for her."

"Doin' what?"

"Why entertainin' people; singin' and dancin' and the like."

I was gettin' more confused by the minute. "You mean sort of like a female minstrel show?" I asked.

That set him off again and I was half mad at him poundin' a lamppost and laughin' like a jackass where everybody could hear him.

About a block from the landing Freeman pushed me through the door of a run-down cafe and told me he'd buy my supper. The place smelled worse'n Fatback's galley, but I didn't say nothin'. After Four-Mile had put away his second piece of custard pie, he pulled the napkin off his neck, belched a couple of times and lit up a big stogie. I tell you, he was the picture of contentment.

"I fetched you along today for two reasons, Peter," he said. "First, 'cause you got the makings of a good clerk. And second, 'cause it's time you was gettin' out on your own and testin' your manhood."

"Where am I gonna test it?"

"Why, at Vicksburg Annie's! There ain't a better place in the world for a young buck to learn the ways of the world. You gotta get your feet wet sometime, don't you? You're mighty lucky to have somebody like me to look after you and see you get back alive."

I remember our preacher said something about the tests of manhood once, only I don't think that's what Four-Mile had in mind. But I didn't press it. "What's Miss Vicksburg the queen of?" I asked.

"Vicksburg ain't really her name, that's the place she won her fame. During the Siege of Vicksburg she was the queen of Grant's army. She took care of the Boys in Blue like they was her very own. She traveled right with 'em and once they assigned a whole cavalry troop to make sure the Rebs didn't harm her. Why Grant would've sooner given up the services of General Sherman than her, that's how much he thought of her."

"She was an army nurse, is that what you're tellin' me?"

"Oh, she was a nurse alright, when there was need, but her biggest job was to keep them soldiers happy and make sure they didn't get homesick."

"How'd she do that?"

"Hell fire, if you ain't about the most innocent babe I ever seen! She made 'em happy by goin' to bed with 'em, that's how! When the war was over, she bought her a boat and got rich runnin' the only floatin' whorehouse on the river. She named it the *Union Victory* and I was one of the first deckhands she ever had. That's how I took up steamboatin' and I ain't never had it so good since. It was a mighty fine boat, let me tell you, only it caught fire at Cape Girardeau a few years back and burned right down to the guards. And that's how Annie come to settle down ashore."

About then there was a long silence. Four-Mile was starin' at me with a funny look in his eye.

"Kid, you sure you know what a whore is?"

"Anybody knows that," I said, gettin' mad because I could feel my neck and ears turnin' red. "A wicked woman, a loose female."

"There's where you're dead wrong," he said, shakin' his cigar in my face. "I'll take a bawdyhouse girl over half the females you meet in church. A whore knows how to treat a man. They ain't spiteful and mean and they don't nag at you, neither."

He had a lot more to say after we got out in the street, only I wasn't listenin' too good because of all the butterflies in my belly. I guess that's what happens when you eat cafe grub. After about three blocks we turned down an alley and picked our way through the mud to the back door of a two-story frame building. There wasn't a light anywhere. If I could've seen where to run, I would've high-tailed it out of there, Freeman or no Freeman.

He fumbled around with a match until he found a rope hangin' inside the door and when he pulled it I could hear a bell jinglin' up above. Then he pointed me up the stairs and every time I slowed down he jabbed me in the rear. He must've thought I wasn't too keen on meetin' his friends. The door opened before I got to the top and there stood a little squirt of a fellow with a bushy mustache and a head as bald as an egg. Four-Mile yelled "Hoppin' Bob!" along with a few other choice terms and told me to shake hands with the last survivin' Black River pirate. I've heard about the Black River boys and how they used to poach logs, but he didn't look much like a pirate to me.

Hoppin' Bob pulled me through the door and I just stood there, not believin' my eyes. The walls were lined with mirrors and fancy paintings in big gilt frames and the carpet on the floor was about ankle deep. Just for a minute I felt like kickin' off my shoes and tryin' it with my bare feet. I counted three green horsehair sofas and six settees, along with a bunch of marbletop tables and some potted plants growin' higher'n a man's head. In the middle of the ceiling was one of those chandeliers about the size of a washtub made out of green glass with gold beads hangin' from the edges. The longest bar I ever saw stretched across the west wall and that's where Hoppin' Bob herded us, all the time jabbering away with Four-Mile. Hangin' on the wall behind the bar was a painting of some fat woman all laid out without a stitch of clothes on. I mean not one stitch. At first I tried not to look, but it was too big to pass up.

All at once Hoppin' Bob's eyes lit up and he pointed across the room. There stood a buxom female only about a half-size smaller'n Freeman. Four-Mile let out a whoop and I knew without anybody tellin' me that was Vicksburg Annie. They grabbed each other and did a little dance in the middle of the room, sort of like two elephants in a circus ring. When Four-Mile spun her around, the whole building shook. I'll bet that woman weighed better'n 200 pounds. Her hair was stacked up in a big pile and her face was painted to a fare-thee-well. She was wearin' a long gown about the color of the sofas and she had about 10 pounds of jewelry hangin' from her neck and ears. I've seen a lot of ugly women, but I never met up with one that had a mustache before. She had a voice like a fog horn and when she patted me on the head and told me what a nice lad I was, I wanted to crawl under the carpet. General Grant didn't need to worry about her; a female like that could whip the whole Confederate Army single-handed.

Four-Mile pointed to a table and when I sat down first he stomped on my foot. I let out a yelp and jumped up, but all I got was one of those mean looks of his. Then he pulled out a chair and waved his arms and made a big to-do about sittin' Annie down. I'd never seen him carry on like that before, that's sure.

Hoppin' Bob came scurryin' along behind us with a bottle of whisky and three glasses. He poured them right to the brim and I knew I was in for it. Annie and Four-Mile hoisted their glasses up high, then they banged them together and swallowed the stuff with one gulp. I never could stand the smell of whisky and I knew the taste would be worse, so I just sat there lookin' at it. But pretty soon I had the feeling Four-Mile was ready to stomp me again, so I held my breath and made a grab for it. It wasn't so bad 'til I tried to get some air in my lungs. You talk about fire! The coals in the *Jessie Bill*'s firebox couldn't be half as hot. I sputtered and carried on like a drownin man and when I tried to find an open window I couldn't see a thing for all the water in my eyes. Right then I swore the next time one of those temperance people came around, I'll take the pledge and gladly.

After I started breathin' again and Freeman stopped beatin' on the table and laughin', a couple of girls sidled up to his chair and started pattin' his hair. Vicksburg Annie stiffened up and they quick-like moved over to me, gigglin' all the time. Annie reeled off their names and told me to shake hands. All that got was more giggles. I couldn't decide which was the homeliest. The tall one was named Evalina and there wasn't much to her besides bones and hair. The other one said her name was Dixie. She was a couple feet shorter and she had muscles like a deckhand.

Four-Mile said we should go sit on the couch and get acquainted and I figured anything was better'n another shot of whisky. Those girls must have been goin' someplace, because they was in an awful hurry to get to know me. They maneuvered around so I was in the middle and both of them started talkin' a blue streak. I didn't pay no attention until I heard Evalina say "I get him first." Then Dixie started tellin' me how young and tender I was and I knew it was time to cast off.

I no more'n got to my feet when Dixie gave my arm a flip and laid me out flat on the couch. And that wasn't all! They were all over me in a wink, one of 'em ticklin' my ribs and the other one mussin' my hair. No man I know ever hit a lady, but these weren't ladies and besides that, I was gettin' madder by the minute. I gave Evalina an elbow in the windpipe and then I came up hard with my head right on Dixie's chin. There was a door on the other side of the room and I went through it with a full head of steam.

It was pretty dark and all I could make out was a long hall with a door every so often. I started to open the second or third one I came to, only the door opened first and I went flyin' inside before I could catch myself, slammin' into another girl. Both of us hit the floor and I didn't know it was a girl until she started screamin' her head off. The trouble was she was carryin' a chamber pot and the things she said even Four-Mile could have learned something. I got out of there fast and I didn't look to see who was comin' after me down the hall, but it sounded like one of those stampedes that Buffalo Bill wrote about once in the *Argus*.

For a minute I thought I was trapped for sure. Then the hall took a hard bend to port and I went for the first doorknob I could get my hands on. This time I shut the door easy-like and I just stood there tryin' to figure out what I was goin' to do next. It was pitch-black so I started edging around the room, feeling my way along the wall. In a little bit I came to the corner and there was another door. It was open a crack and from the apple smell I figured it must be a storeroom. I was afraid the door would squeak so I left it alone and started along the wall again, hopin' I'd find a window. I did, too, and I guess you could say that's when all heck busted loose. The window was stuck and when I stepped back to give it a heave, I hit something and went over backwards, makin' enough racket to wake the dead and bangin' my head against a bed rail. Some dame let out an awful scream and there was a big thrashin' of bedclothes and a man's voice yellin' something in between screams.

The next thing I knew two boots hit the floor. I should say only one, because the other'n hit me and when I felt those spikes I lunged under the bed like a mouse goin' for his hole. Everybody knows those lumberjacks are crazy, but I didn't think they wore their boots to bed.

From then on things went from bad to worse. The dame let off screamin' long enough to holler "The candle! Light the candle!" The lumberjack was stompin' around sayin' "My britches, where in blazes are my britches?" The door came flyin' open and all the people who'd been chasin' me tried to wedge their way into the room. By turning my head a little, I could see Hoppin' Bob holding a lamp and tryin' to keep from bein' run over. People were shovin' from behind and the lumberjack was wavin' a long knife and makin' like he was going to carve up the whole crowd if they didn't get out of his room and let him get his britches on.

That lamp was something I didn't care for, or the knife, either, for that matter. But as long as things were in an uproar, I knew I still had a chance, so I headed for the storeroom as fast as I could crawl. This time I found a window right off and below it was a nice flat roof. There was freedom starin' me right in the face, only that blasted sash wouldn't budge no matter how hard I tugged. I knew there wasn't any help for it, so I grabbed a butter churn off the floor and gave it a big heave. I hit the roof right behind the churn and it was all I could do to keep from goin' over the edge.

I don't think I've ever been in such a terrible bind. I was hangin' by my fingers and tryin' to get my legs wrapped around a corner post when people started poppin' out of that window like hornets. You never heard such a commotion. I couldn't decide whether to slide or jump when I heard a loud cracking noise, like when a boat busts a spar trying to get off a sandbar. Everything was dead still for a second or two and then there was an awful rumbling sound and the whole porch let go.

You couldn't imagine a bigger mess, even if I could describe it. There was mud and flying shingles and busted boards and people were layin' all over the ground, groanin' and cussin'. Just as I was pickin' myself up, somebody bumped into me and there stood Dixie with her hair hangin' in her face and mud from top to bottom. "Lover lad!" she shouted, and then she made a grab for me, but all she got was an armful of air.

I never stopped runnin' until I hit the levee.

Chapter Six

Most people in the river towns
were of the opinion that rafting was
but a diversion for the crews; their
true calling was battle, murder and
sudden death. It was a fact that when
a raft tied up at Guttenberg Bend the
widow Fowler hid her silver spoons.
—Walter Havighurst

MAY 7, 1880:

Poets are an uncommon lot on the river and I suppose that's why Cleve Allen goes against the Bible and keeps his light hid under a bushel. At least that's what I call it when he scribbles those verses on the back of old lading bills and then squirrels 'em away under his straw tick. If they was mine, I'd probably want the whole world to know about it. But Cleve is touchy and he keeps tellin' me what he'll do if I ever tell anybody on the *Jessie Bill.*

"Words keep runnin' through my head, sort of like music," he told me once. "I don't get any peace until I get off by myself and take a pencil to 'em. It's a burden, let me tell you." Mostly he writes about the river and the way the sky looks after a storm or how a doe brings her fawn down to drink after sundown. Some of 'em rhyme and some of 'em don't—and some of 'em he won't even let me read. He can write sad and he can write funny. I like the funny ones best, especially one or two about the captain. I laugh until the tears come every time.

People like Wabasha Dan and Four-Mile, they got a feel for the river, but not like Cleve's. Sometimes at night he'll try and tell me about it and I think I understand—sort of like the way Ma feels when she sits in church. To tell the truth, Cleve's not a very good second mate. But he's a fine steersman and he can already handle a boat a lot better than the captain.

Cleve was about my age when he took to the river; he'll be 26 his next birthday. He's some taller'n me and he has what you'd call rusty hair and a beard that he cuts real short. You think he's skinny when you first look at him, but he's got good shoulders and a lot of strength in his arms. And he needs it, the way the girls flock around when he goes ashore. Girls are about the only thing that scare him and Four-Mile keeps calling it "a crime against nature"—whatever that is.

Cleve grew up around McGregor. His house was up on the bluff south of town almost on the very spot where Zebulon Pike and his soldiers camped way back when this was a foreign country with nothin' but Indians and a few Britishers and Frenchmen and Spaniards all arguin' over who owned it. Maybe that's why Cleve knows so much about history—a whale of a lot more'n Professor Howe, it seems to me. Once Cleve told me he could sit up there on the bluff all by hisself and see Joliet and Marquette come paddling out of the Wisconsin River just like they did in 1673. Mind you, he even described the look on their faces when it dawned on them they was the first white men to see the Upper Mississippi. Cap'n Lafe could never do that, even with a five-gallon jug of wine.

I like to think I'm beginning to see the river a little like Cleve does. Only I can't describe it near as well. Cleve's right when he says there's no stillness in this world like the stillness on the river just before first light. I like to watch the fog the way it smokes and drips sometimes over the raft. There are times when the mist gets inside your bones when you stand shiverin' on the guards and watch the bank go slidin' by maybe no more'n 10 feet away. You hear a redwing blackbird callin' in the willows and when the sky begins to redden up a little, you might spot a beaver swim-

min' alongside. I've never seen a beaver yet that couldn't make
better time than the *Jessie Bill*.

At night the river is a different world, let me tell you. Once in
a while I crawl up on the lazy bench when Cleve is steerin' for
Wabasha Dan. Then when Dan takes the wheel to make a crossing, the two of us'll walk out to the head of the raft instead of goin'
to our bunks. The stars seem to move down until they're not much
higher than the bluffs. A whippoorwill will let go somewhere
close and two or three more will pick it up over on the other side of
the river. You hear the water slappin' against the logs and when you
come into a bend you see nothin' but big black shadows comin'
straight at you and you wonder if Wabasha Dan maybe waited
too long. Then just at the last minute the whole thing swings back
into the starlight. When you look back over your shoulder all you
can see are the running lights winking on the chimneys and then
you know why they say ol' Dan has got eyes better'n any cat.

But I wouldn't want anybody to get the idea I spend my time
lollygaggin' in the pilothouse or sittin' out on the raft countin'
stars. Bein' short-handed like we are, it's a rare thing when you
get a minute of peace on this ol' tub. After we got the second
piece of our raft hitched in and started downriver, Cap'n Lafe
and Pot Belly kept me on the jump. For once I didn't complain,
because after that mess at Vicksburg Annie's place, all I wanted
to do was give Four-Mile a wide berth.

He never said one word about what happened at Wabasha, but
I was sure he was smokin' under the collar over the way I made a
fool of myself in front of all his friends. Those are the kind of
friends I can do without—especially Evalina and Dixie. I still
don't know if Four-Mile was out on that porch roof when it col-
lapsed. I reckon he was because his face was all scratched up and
he limped around for two or three days, givin' the rousters Holy
Ned whether they did anything wrong or not.

It took the better part of a day to get the raft all trim and
square and it was three o'clock Sunday afternoon before we left
Alma on a falling river. The weather was clear and everybody
was in a good mood—except Four Mile. It was dusk by the time
we got to West Newton and we had to wait a spell for two rafts
sittin' side by side and takin' up almost the whole river.

The *Governor Thomas* had one and the *Kentucky Racer* had the other and there was a lot of shoutin' back and forth. The rafting works at West Newton is a lot smaller than the one at Beef Slough and Four-Mile says it's a sloppy operation. They don't have enough slack water for one thing and when their boats are gettin' all tied in, they liked to hog the whole channel just to irritate those who do business up at Beef Slough.

The *Thomas* moved out first and we swung in behind the *Kentucky Racer* like we was planning to run over her. The truth is the *Jessie Bill* couldn't run over anything bigger'n a jonboat and the *Racer*'s running lights was out of sight in less than an hour.

We raised Minneiska about half past ten and I decided to get a little sleep before we got to Chimney Rock—just in case. At low stage there's at least five places between Alma and Dresbach where a raft boat can get in trouble. Some rafters won't run 'em at night, but that don't bother Wabasha Dan—unless there's heavy fog.

I woke up a little after midnight and when I heard Dan give the engine room a slow bell I figured he was comin' into Chimney Rock crossing. The trick is to keep out of the shoal water by layin' in close to the Minnesota bank. I got to the pilot-house just as Dan gave her full bell and swung the head of the raft hard to port. The boat shuddered a little, but he drove her over the bar in good shape and he had plenty of rudder so the raft could swing with the current as it sweeps under Chimney Rock. If you pick the wrong place to start your crossing or take it at the wrong angle, the shoal water'll grab you and you can sit there and watch that current under the bluff tear the raft right off the buttin' block.

It must have been one o'clock or better when we headed into Betsey Bend Slough and Wabasha Dan didn't waste any time decidin' we'd have to "back the bend." Everybody on watch was sure he'd take her through, but Dan ain't one to argue when the river tells him he's gonna have to run her the hard way. Right in the middle of the slough, the channel turns back on itself to make the meanest bend on the upper river. When there's plenty of water, you can make it by swinging to the outside and holding her nose in the willows. But when the gauge is down, you got two choices—double trip or back the bend.

Most raft people would sooner lose a month's pay than go to all the work of double-trippin'. You have to stop and undo all those lines so you can split the raft into two pieces. You take it through one piece at a time and then hitch it all back up again.

Backin' the bend is a little easier than that, but it's mighty tricky at night. You head into the bend as far as you dare, keepin' in mind that nobody has yet figured out how to put brakes on a boat. Then you give her a backin' bell and, as Cleve says, you start prayin'. Pretty soon the buckets start churnin' backwards and the boat shakes right down to her planking, but she keeps right on slidin' forward. Every foot puts you closer to the bank; but about the time the hair starts to stand up on the back of your neck, she slowly loses headway and eases to a stop. Then's when you think the ol' girl is gonna pull herself inside out, but she starts backin' ever so slow, groanin' every inch of the way. Wabasha Dan, of course, makes it look easy as pie. Now he gives the raft a good nudge with the steam nigger. After that he rings for Pot Belly to come ahead and we're standin' down the river like it was broad daylight.

Winona Bar is another place with a bad reputation and I've heard Four-Mile tell about the time he counted 11 boats either aground or waitin' to get over. Dan eased her off some, but it didn't take him long to find the water he needed and we were across before the after watch came up for breakfast.

We made Trempealeau by half past eleven and by two o'clock we had scraped over the bar at Queen's Bluff and made the run down Hammond Chute, leavin' nothin' but easy water all the way to Dresbach. It started to rain some when we passed the mouth of the Black River at sundown and there was a patch of fog here and there when we raised LaCrosse along about eight o'clock. We was close to Brownsville when I finally got to bed and I never so much as twitched until I heard the breakfast bell. That's one bell a man never wants to miss.

At first I thought it was Fatback's grub that had everybody upset, but it was no worse'n usual. Finally I got the bad news from Cleve. Wabasha Dan and the captain got into it when we were comin' out of Coon Slough. Nobody knew for sure what started it, but Dan went stompin' out of the pilothouse and announced he was gettin' off at the next wood stop.

Ol' Lafe said it couldn't be too soon to suit him and instead of callin' Cleve, he took the wheel hisself, ravin' and shoutin' that he didn't need a rum-soaked pilot to get the *Jessie Bill* to Fort Madison. Then Four-Mile tried bein' the peacemaker and that only made things worse. In fact, he got so shook up he forgot he was mad at me.

When Cap'n Lafe is at the helm, people start carryin' on in strange ways. You'd thought it was the day before doomsday. Bush McDonald quit runnin' off at the mouth and Limber Jim Gray and the rest of the rousters stood around up on the front end lookin' kind of wild-eyed. Ercel Waters went so far as to throw away his rabbit's foot when we headed into Bad Axe Bend, but we came through in good shape and except for one or two spots, there wasn't much to get jumpy about between there and Lansing. By the middle of the afternoon I began to think ol' Lafe wasn't such a bad pilot after all, but I didn't dare say it. Everybody relaxed some and Cleve, he even slipped off and took a nap.

I guess you could say that was the lull before the storm. In fact, it was tryin' to cook up a little storm all the way from Atafalaya Bluff to the head of Crooked Slough. Clouds kept buildin' up in the west and there was some lightning behind them. Maybe it was the weather, or maybe it was the sight of another raft bearin' down behind us. Anyway, the captain all of a sudden had his hands full with two sharp bends comin' up and what looked to be the crazy *Crescent City* on his tail.

Crooked Slough is right at five miles from head to foot and there ain't a friendly piece of water in it. The sandbars keep hoppin' around and you won't catch one in the same place twice. The captain don't like to play that kind of tag and the way he was janglin' the engine bell, it was hard to tell where one signal left off and the next one began.

We was feelin' our way into the second bend when a long whistle blast froze my feet right to the deck. For an instant, I thought it was some smart-ass stunt by the *Crescent City*, but the tone wasn't right and neither was the direction. Then there was a second blast longer than the first and I knew it had to be an upstream packet. It was the *Milwaukee* and she could see the head of our raft before we could see her.

Some say the captain panicked and gave the engine room a full bell instead of a stoppin' bell. And some say he would've been alright if he hadn't fed the wheel a few too many spokes to port. All I know is there was a terrible jolt and all of Fatback's pots and pans went flyin' around the galley. I picked myself up in time to see the front corner of the raft lift out of the water and head for some farmer's cowshed on the Wisconsin bank. Lines were poppin' like fiddlestrings. As soon as we stopped, the current carried us sideways and hung us on a bar on the Iowa side of the channel. There was the *Milwaukee* and it was almost funny to see her backin' water like crazy tryin' to get out of the road. Upriver the *Crescent City* was also doin' some scrambling of her own. By the time she got stopped, the head of her raft wasn't more'n 75 yards off our stern.

Everybody knows the *Jessie Bill*'s reputation for gettin' into messes, but this time we outdid ourselves. There we was pluggin' up the whole river like the corncob in the captain's wine jug. Our raft was strung out like some dying thing. It was split down the middle with the front end of the portside piece draped over the bank and loose logs swingin' and bobbin' away with the current. The starboard piece was still hangin' together, but it was all bent out of shape and the front end was slowly driftin' over toward the *Milwaukee*.

It wasn't long 'til Four-Mile was bellowin' like a bull, calling for all hands. The first thing he did was to get the yawl in the river and send three rousters downstream to try and jury-rig some kind of sheer-boom to catch the runaway logs. Then he put everybody else out on the starboard piece to try and keep it from breakin' up. Bush and I scrambled around to find new line and all the other stuff he was yellin' for. By then it had started to rain and the light was failin' fast. The rain kept pickin' up speed and by the time I rounded up all the lanterns and got 'em lit, it was comin' down in buckets.

About nine o'clock Erin Murphy and a couple of others came along side in the *Crescent City* yawl. The water was runnin' out of Murphy's beard in a stream and he was smartin' off something fierce, wantin' to know if we had anything on this boat besides idiots and when we planned to give the river back to them that know how to use it. As soon as he saw Four-Mile, he quieted down in a hurry. Four-Mile didn't explode like I thought he would. He just stood there for a minute, then he hooked a finger in the front of Murphy's coat. "You ought'n to be out in this rain without your hat, Murphy. Your brain's liable to shrink some more. We've done about all we can do tonight and as soon as you send some men over to help in the mornin', we'll give you back the river."

And that's the way it was, too—thanks to all that rain. We must have had a good three inches during the night and Pot Belly thought there'd be enough of a rise to get us off the bar. The *Crescent City* sent over five men at daylight and Four-Mile set 'em to patchin' up what was left of the portside piece. As soon as we got steam up, he put a line on the steam nigger and swung the starboard piece back into position. Then he cut it loose and the rousters got out in front in the yawl and started herdin' it through the bend. The *Crescent City* men dropped the stub piece in behind and the current did the rest.

I hadn't given a thought to Wabasha Dan, but there he was back in the pilothouse like nothin' had ever happened. He rang the engine room to come ahead slow, then he gave a backing bell. At first we didn't budge. You could feel the old girl shake and quiver under foot and the wheel began to churn up a storm of mud and sand. Then there was a little motion, first forward and then back, in answer to Dan's bells. A little later she gave a lurch and we were free. Hallelujah!

About a half mile downriver we caught up with the starboard piece and eased it up to the buttin' block. Four-Mile put on just enough line to hold her and as soon as we could, we laid it up against the Iowa bank and snubbed it tight to a couple of big sycamores. The *Crescent City* rousters had the little piece tied off on the other bank and it was plain we weren't going to get any more work out of them. Four-Mile had rigged a holding pen for loose logs when the *Crescent City* came down about ten to pick up her men. Murphy was hangin' out the pilothouse shakin' his fist and the way he was usin' the whistle, every blast was a cuss word.

It was different with the *Milwaukee*. She turned around after we went aground and we figured she went back to Lynxville to tie up for the night and let off any passengers who were havin' fits because of the delay. As soon as we got the logs out of the channel, she headed upriver, all proud and snooty, never even givin' us a second look. I felt like sayin' we was sorry for what happened, but when she didn't even so much as whistle, I changed my mind. You can say what you want about the *Jessie Bill*, but she don't cotton to an uppity packet boat.

We spent the rest of Wednesday roundin' up logs in every slough and backwater between Lynxville and Jackson Island. It was a man-killin' job, too, with the river risin' like it was. We had to build a new crib for the portside piece and the only time I slowed down was to fill the lanterns again so we could see to run the lines and get everything back in shape.

I was so pooped the next mornin' I didn't even bother to go ashore when we put in for fuel at Dee's Woodyard below McGregor. Ol' Man Dee must be about the meanest man on the upper river and nobody does business with him unless they have to. He's got a pack of dogs just as mean as him and a rifle which he keeps handy in case anybody tries to get friendly with his daughter, Mary. Up and down the river, they call her the Corn-Fed Gal. She's supposed to be a ravin' beauty and the trick is to get a look at her without gettin' bit or shot. The catch is nobody's seen her for years, at least no rafter that I ever talked to. If the truth was known, I don't think he ever had a daughter, let alone one that was corn-fed.

We were abreast of the Dubuque Shot Tower when the breakfast bell rang Friday morning and we cleared Bellevue Slough without a hitch before they called the afternoon watch. Fog caught us before daylight Saturday and you could barely make out the lights of Clinton, but Wabasha Dan hardly slowed down except for the crossing at the head of Beaver Island.

By the time we raised Princeton, I was a little jumpy knowin' that LeClaire was just around the bend. I didn't let on, but I halfway expected to see Marshal Raintree hailin' us with one of his muskets and a warrant for my arrest. But there was only two boats at the landing and nobody gave us a second look except for three or four raftsmen sittin' around a fire at the Green Tree Hotel. All the same, I was glad we didn't have to land and pick up a pilot to get through the rapids. Wabasha Dan wouldn't let a rapids pilot on board if he could help it and whenever Cap'n Lafe thought we ought to have one, Dan always settled it by tellin' him how much money he'd save.

Cleve Allen and I were out on the raft when we cleared Campbell's Island and we could feel the current tryin' to push us to starboard. "You see that?" he pointed. "That spells trouble when we double-trip through the Rock Island bridge." I groaned a little because double-trippin' means nothin' but hard work, even when there's no current. There are eight bridges between Beef Slough and Fort Madison, but Rock Island is the one that rafters cuss the most. Pot Belly can go on about that bridge for ten minutes and he always starts off the same way. "The invention of Satan and the Rock Island Railroad," he calls it.

Cleve said the railroad didn't know any better when they set the piers at an angle to the current. When the river stage is above eight feet, you better mind your business or that bridge will reach out and grab you. I guess that's where Satan comes into it. People still talk about how the *Effie Alton* and the *Gray Eagle* and several others smashed into the piers and sunk. Professor Howe showed me some clippings once about the *Effie Alton* and I wished he hadn't, because it sure opened my eyes about Abe Lincoln. That was in 1856 when the bridge was new and the *Alton*'s owners didn't think it should have been there in the first place. So they sued the Rock Island Railroad for damages. But they never collected a red cent. The railroad hired Lincoln as their lawyer and he won the case. And ever since, the railroads been lordin' it over every boat on the river. When you think what a great man Lincoln was, you wonder how he got mixed up with the railroad people. But then I guess everybody makes mistakes and I'm not one to blame a man for something he did when he was young and foolish.

When we heard Wabasha Dan give a slow bell, Cleve and I hustled back to the boat deck to get ready to land above the bridge and tie off one piece of the raft. A stopping bell followed and as we eased into the Illinois bank, we started backing, just enough to kill our headway so the rousters could make the head of the raft fast to a tree.

Cleve was ready to go to work when Four-Mile waved him off with a grin. "We're gonna make a double-header," he yelled. "Dan says he can take her through and I ain't one to argue." Cleve looked like he wasn't hearin' right and Pot Belly came runnin' out on deck, shakin' a Stillson wrench and shoutin' that every last one of us would be drowned.

As for me, I wasn't even sure what a double-header was, but I could tell it was gonna be exciting. In no time at all, Dan maneuvered the boat over against the outside piece. Then we started to back, easy-like, while Four-Mile let go the coupling lines. The inside piece floated free and when the stern end cleared the head of the outside piece, we were all there to swing it into line and make it fast.

Then down the river we went on a full bell, a half raft wide and two rafts long! I could feel the current speed us along and just for a minute, when the bridge came into sight, I had some kindly thoughts about Professor Howe's schoolroom. All of a sudden, Cleve looked a little pale and he wasn't much interested in my questions. "A double-header is something you do in slack water," he said. "With current like this, I'd sooner go over Niagara Falls in a barrel."

Dan gave the *Jessie Bill* a hard right rudder, driving her toward the Davenport bank. Then he eased her off, lettin' the head of the raft swing into the middle of the channel. Strung out like it was, the raft bent and twisted in the water like an oversized snake. We were closin' fast now and Cleve was gettin' more nervous by the minute. "He's got to straighten her out," he said, mostly talkin' to himself. The closer those black piers got, the worse my stomach felt. We were being pulled along behind a runaway raft and I couldn't see any help for it.

The boat began to flank some and that meant Dan was using his left rudder. But I couldn't see that it was helpin' any, the way the head of the raft was drivin' straight for the starboard pier. I wanted to yell but the words got stuck in my throat. Then just at the last second the head end seemed to jump free, and we were into the draw span—slick as a whistle!

Four-Mile and all the rousters ran out on the raft where Dan could see 'em from the pilothouse and gave him a big cheer. I looked for the captain, but he wasn't in sight and I didn't much blame him. If he ever needed a little wine to quiet his heart, this was the time.

I kept waitin' for us to make a landing somewhere, but just above Credit Island, Four-Mile called for all hands and we cut the forward piece loose and eased it back into position—still standin' down the river, mind you. Then we coupled up the two pieces and for a few minutes the whole blamed raft floated free while Dan got the boat back on the buttin' block and all tied in again.

I tell you, it was just about the slickest operation I'd ever seen. Nobody but Wabasha Dan Wilson could beat Satan and the Rock Island Railroad all in one day.

Chapter Seven

THE RAFTSMAN
He never shaved the whiskers
From off his horny hide;
He drove them in with hammers
And chawed them off inside.

MAY 17, 1880:

There for a while I was beginnin' to think the *Jessie Bill* would be laid up at Fort Madison all summer. I got nothin' against the town, but when you have engine trouble and a mutiny on your hands with half the crew threatening to quit, it can unsettle a man.

We aimed to make Fort Madison by Monday night, but we blowed a joint below Burlington and it was Tuesday afternoon before we delivered the raft to the Atlee yards. Cap'n Lafe was happy as a lark and he couldn't wait to pack his carpetbag and get over to the Anthes Hotel for a bath and a haircut. I routed him out of bed about nine the next morning and when we got to the Atlee office to settle up, he still smelled like a walkin' wine barrel.

The captain knew we weren't gonna get any premium money because it took us nine days comin' down instead of six, but he was mighty put out when they docked us for losin' logs. Our Beef Slough manifest showed six brails totaling 4,966 logs, but the Atlee yard foreman said our break-up in Crooked Slough left us 251 logs shy. Lafe is not one to take a thing like that layin' down. He raved a while and upset an inkwell pounding on the table, but it didn't do a bit of good. They made out a check for $598.50 and told him to take it or leave it; after another threat or two, he took it.

You'd think that'd be enough financial troubles for one day, but it wasn't hardly a start. Some dandy wearin' a green velvet vest and a checkered suit followed us out of the Atlee office and started pumpin' the captain's hand like a long-lost brother. Ol' Lafe took one look and his face turned the color of the fellow's vest. I never did catch his name, but I knew what his game was as soon as he said something about the Farmers Savings Bank of Davenport and a $250.00 promissory note that was overdue— two months to be exact.

The thing that got me was the way this dude carried on, just as pleasant as pie. Never once did he stop smilin'. "I'll be happy to drive you to the bank, Captain Clapsaddle," he said, pointing to a surrey tied across the street. "When you cash your check, I know you'll want to take care of this note, plus interest, of course, and my travel expenses from Davenport. Let me say it was a thrill to watch your boat make a spectacular run through the Rock Island bridge the other day. I wouldn't have missed it for the world."

By this time, Lafe had lost all of his fight and he climbed into the surrey like a man goin' to the gallows. "Meet Mr. Collins," our banker friend said, nodding toward the driver. "He's the deputy sheriff of Lee County and he is prepared to attach your boat, but I have assured him this won't be necessary." The captain's eyes were glassy and I don't think he heard a word that was bein' said.

When we got back to the landing, the crew was all washed and combed and waitin' on the forecastle for their pay. The captain whizzed past them like they had the plague and then they all set on me with everybody talkin' at once. Pretty soon Four-Mile came down the stairs with the captain in tow, both of 'em looking grim. The weather was on the cool side, but Lafe kept moppin' his face with a handkerchief and fightin' a frog in his throat. At first he could hardly talk, but he soon got warmed up tellin' us how the bankers was bleedin' him and takin' the food right out of the mouths of all the loyal people who believed in him and the *Jessie Bill*.

Finally Pot Belly started wavin' his hand in the captain's face. "Dang it, Clapsaddle, are you tryin' to tell us we ain't gettin' paid?"

Lafe looked put out. "It was my intention to pay all hands in full and have a little left over for the owners. But all of us will have to tighten our belts."

"Hell, my belt's in the last notch now," Grumble Jones called out. "You owe us three months pay and I ain't settling for less."

"I'm well aware of what you have coming," the captain said. He tried to stick out his chest, but it was mostly belly that moved. "I have a simple proposition to make to you men: one month's pay now and the rest when we bring down the next raft."

"I've heard that tune once too often," Pot Belly snorted. "Only this time I ain't dancin'. Full pay or this boat don't leave the landing."

Right about then is when the weather started warmin' up.

"That's mutiny!" the captain screamed. "This time you've gone too far, Carmichael. You're fired! Get off my boat!"

"You can't fire a man without payin' him off," Pot Belly shot back. "Even if you could, you'd have to hire me back. The shape this ol' bucket of bolts is in, she'd never make it upriver again. And I'm the only man who can fix her. That's where I got you, Clapsaddle."

Late in the afternoon the captain called me up to his cabin and announced there'd be two months pay for all hands instead of just one. Wabasha Dan was the first to draw his and he never said a word when I counted it out. Four-Mile had a few things to say about the captain, but he took his and disappeared and so did Cleve. Mudcat Lewis and Limber Jim Gray stood outside the cabin and argued for most of a half hour, finally deciding to take what they could get and risk collecting the rest later.

But not Pot Belly. I could see him down on the boat deck with Grumble Jones, Ercel Waters, Pinhead Grant and Argonaut Smith all huddled around him. Bush McDonald and Fatback was there, too, and the way Pot Belly was bendin' their ears, I knew I might as well put the money back in the safe.

The next day everybody just sat around and looked at each other without sayin' a word. Ol' Lafe was pacing around his cabin and finally he called for Mudcat Lewis and told him he'd make him the engineer and raise his pay if he could repack the joint and get steam up. Not wanting to be second fireman the rest of his life, Mudcat allowed he'd try if some of the others would give him a hand. As soon as the captain and Mudcat started down the stairs, the whole boat came alive. Everybody made a bee-line for the deckhouse and for a minute or so, things was dead-quiet with each bunch starin' at the other, not more'n three feet apart.

Mudcat took a step toward the engine room, but before he hardly got his foot planted, Grumble Jones slammed him up against the bulkhead. "Nobody touches them engines 'til Pot Belly gives the word," Grumble said in a testy voice. Mudcat puffed up like a peacock and threw an armlock on Grumble's neck. Both sides rushed in and there would have been one terrible ruckus if Four-Mile hadn't started grabbin' people and shovin' them—some to starboard and some to port. Four-Mile was mad, let me tell you, and that's when you don't want to so much as look at him cross-eyed. He just stood there, breathin' hard, and it wasn't too long until everybody sort of tip-toed away—me included.

Cleve Allen was worried about the strike and didn't want to talk, so I went to bed early that night. Sometime during the after watch—if there'd been an after watch—I heard voices and a lot of racket and for a minute I thought there was another fight down on deck. Then I heard some sour singin' and I figured Limber Jim and some of the others had laid one on in some Fort Madison saloon. I was sure Four-Mile must be spendin' the night ashore, because he wouldn't put up with that for one minute. One of the voices was Argonaut Smith's. Just before I dropped off to sleep again, I hard pulleys squeaking and I knew somebody was working the boom on the forecastle.

Another strange thing happened the next morning when two men came up the plank and stood there talkin' with Four-Mile. I was pretty sure one of 'em was the deputy sheriff who drove me and the captain to the bank. After a while Four-Mile led them aft and they went sniffin' around and over everything like a pack of bloodhounds.

Finally they left and Four-Mile stood at the head of the stage until they was off the levee and out of sight. Then he whistled like he does with two fingers and all the deck crew gathered around just by force of habit.

Four-Mile had his hands on his hips and that's a bad sign.

"Where is it, Gray?" he bellowed and everybody jumped, most of all Limber Jim.

"Where's what?"

"The cannon!"

"What cannon? You crazy, Four-Mile? There ain't no cannon on this boat."

"Gray, wasn't you an artilleryman?"

"Yeah."

"And haven't you been blowin' about how you was the best gunner in Billy Sherman's army?"

"Well, maybe I did."

"Then, by God, who else would be dumb enough and drunk enough to steal a cannon?"

"It ain't no cannon! It's a mountain howitzer. As slick a gun as you ever seen. Made me sick to see it sittin' there in the courthouse yard. Why, that piece ain't had no care in years."

Four-Mile was shakin' his head. "You haven't answered my question. Where is it?"

"You mean you ain't found it?"

"No, but I'm gonna start by takin' your hide off."

"It's under the woodpile. Way back out of the way."

"Just tell me one more thing: how in hell did you get it aboard?"

"Why, it wasn't no trick a-tall. It comes apart easy as pie. Three mules can pack one all day and never get up a sweat. The tube ain't even three feet long and don't weigh but about two hundred pounds. After that there's only the carriage and a couple of wheels. Soon as I seen it, I said to myself 'There's something no self-respectin' steamboat should be without.' Argonaut and Mudcat, they agreed with me after I explained it to 'em and we hired a dray. Why everything was out in the open. Two or three fellows gathered 'round to watch and they was good enough to help us load it. You call that stealin'?"

Limber Jim stood silent for a minute and a big frown came across his face. "You gonna make me take it back?" he asked. Four-Mile never said a word but he looked like he wanted to stuff Limber Jim down the barrel of that gun—head first. He just shoved his hands in his pockets and stomped off.

Pot Belly knew he had ol' Lafe where the hair was short and everyday his price for settlin' the strike got higher. The captain got so he wouldn't talk to him and you could see there was gonna be a big blow-up. There would've been, too, if Lulu—bless her heart—hadn't showed up.

I never knew a woman could be so fat. She had to be more'n 200 pounds, but it didn't slow her down none. And she wasn't backward, either. Everybody got out of her road, includin' Four-Mile. But I'm gettin' ahead of myself. I was washin' windows in the pilothouse on Tuesday morning when I saw her come drivin' up in a little buckboard. She looked the boat over for a minute or two and then she started yellin' "Oakleeee! Oakleeee Carmichael!" Her voice was like a busted bugle.

From that minute on, Pot Belly was a beaten man. At first I couldn't figure out who she was, but when I went below and saw the look on Pot Belly's face and heard everybody laughin', I knew she had to be his wife. She came up the plank and went straight for Pot Belly like a homing pigeon, talkin' a streak all the way.

"There you are, you weasel of a husband! What do you mean, laying up here in Fort Madison when you're only seven miles from home? You forgot the way to Dallas City? My old mother told me I'd rue the day I married a steamboatman. And I have, too, rest her soul. How do you expect me to keep body and soul together when you're never home? The cow's half sick and I don't even have all the garden in yet...."

There was more, a heap more. Poor ol' Pot Belly took it for as long as he could. "Be still, woman!" he croaked. "What'll these men think of you? Can't you see there's work to be done on this boat? Time's a-wastin' and we've got to get back upriver. Ever'day we sit here is costin' us all money."

Before Lulu could wind up again, Pot Belly started backin' away. "I need two men in the engine room!" he shouted. "If you expect me to fix that joint, I'll have to have some help." All of a sudden that boat was like a beehive. People were whoopin' and cheerin' and even Bush McDonald was happy to have something to do after all that sittin' around.

With Pot Belly givin' orders, Grumble Jones and Mudcat Lewis must've set some kind of a speed record for repacking the starboard joint. It's really not much of a trick when you know how. When the packing around the cylinder head gets a little loose, steam pressure gets behind it and out she comes. It don't hurt nothin', except you got free steam all over the engine room and precious little left to drive the pitmans.

They finished the job in less than an hour, but Pot Belly was afraid to quit, knowin' Lulu was still on board, so he opened the drain cocks and said we'd clean the boilers. Now that's the dirtiest job on the boat and he wouldn't have had much help if it hadn't been for Four-Mile crackin' the whip. He had Ercel Waters and me down under the firebox scrapin' out the mud drum and you never seen such a mess. I don't know how them boilers got any water at all. It was so hot and dirty down there you could scarce breathe. The only thing worse was diggin' out the ash well in front of the fire doors and it did me good to see the sweat roll off Bush McDonald's fat face.

Mrs. Carmichael simmered down when the captain invited her to stay for dinner. He kept shovin' Fatback's vittles at her and once she even smiled when he told her everybody knew her husband was the best engineer on the upper river, bar none. Along in the middle of the afternoon the captain escorted Lulu back to her wagon. Pot Belly was all grease and sweat, but he tore himself away from his work long enough to tell her goodbye. He had the captain give her some money and he promised he'd be home as soon as we came down with the next raft.

Pot Belly and the captain were all smiles when they came back up the plank, like nothin' had ever happened. The whole thing seemed fishy to me, but I couldn't get anybody to talk about it, least of all Cleve Allen.

Before we turned in that night, I asked him point-blank: "Cleve, you ever been to Dallas City?"

He was slow to answer. "Yeah, once."

"When was that?"

"Never mind."

"Cleve, do you think Pot Belly was tricked? How'd his wife know we was here?"

"Peter, if I had to answer all your questions, I'd never get anything else done. Now go to sleep."

Chapter Eight

One thing certain: you can't
make a pilot out of anybody;
a man has to have it born in him;
pilotin' comes natural.
　　　　　　—Frederick Way, Jr.

MAY 22, 1880:

The ol' girl was purrin' like a kitten when we pulled out of Fort Madison and Pot Belly got all the credit for it, deserved or not. I'm talkin' about the *Jessie Bill* and the way she went standin' up the river without any of her usual aches and pains. We was under the Burlington bridge a little after sun-up and we raised New Boston before the light began to fail.

"A little fixin' here and there sure does wonders," Cleve said when we went on watch. I was glad to see him in such a good mood. Matter of fact, everybody was in good spirits and there was no grumblin' when word got around that the captain had decided to pass up Beef Slough and try our luck at Stillwater, up on the St. Croix. I guess he figured we'd have a better chance gettin' a raft and that was fine with me. "Never miss a chance to see new country, 'specially if it don't cost nothin'," Pa used to say.

The river was holdin' steady and the weather was mostly the kind you'd expect if you ordered it and paid cash for it. There was a patch of fog or two of an early morning, but never enough to be bothersome. We lost a little time at Smith's Woodyard while the captain wasted his breath hagglin' about prices. He swears those people can pile wood so ten cords look like thirteen. We had to tie up for a couple of hours when the *Mollie Whitmore* got her raft crossways while makin' the bend at the head of Big Soupbone Island. We also had a little trouble with a contrary sandbar in Deadman's Slough above the mouth of the Fever River, but by noon on Thursday we was sailin' past the Beef Slough closin' boom and that was a good 24 hours better'n we ever done it before.

Fog finally caught us above Wabasha and I wasn't surprised because the whole trip had been too easy. I knew Dan was pushin' to make Read's Landing, but it didn't worry me none because this was his home country and he ought to be able to do it blindfolded. And that's exactly the way it looked to me when I tip-toed into the pilothouse and climbed up on the bench. The way Dan was climbin' the wheel, I knew we was into a bend somewhere. He cocked his head a few times and then he leaned out the window as far as he could. I couldn't hear a thing at first, then I caught it, too—the faraway notes of a calliope.

There's nothin' like the sound of a steam piano to put new life into a raft boat; inside of two minutes every last crew member was out on deck straining to pick up the notes like they was diamonds or rubies. A calliope means a showboat and a showboat means girls and both are pretty rare items, 'specially in these parts.

The music stopped and for the next hour or so there wasn't a sound except the soft breathin' of the *Jessie Bill*'s 'scape pipes. Finally Dan rang a slow bell and we eased into the Read's Landing levee and tied up behind the *Abner Gile*, a dinky little sternwheeler out of Trempealeau. I decided to pass up supper to do a little explorin' and I'd hardly hit the bank when the calliope tuned up again—loud and clear! It was the "Blue Alsatian Mountains" and it sent the chills up my back, let me tell you. My ears took me right to the source, not 50 yards away. It was the *Prairie Flower* and I had a hard time readin' her name board in all the fog. She was about as rough lookin' as the *Jessie Bill* and you'd never give her a second look if it wasn't for the calliope, mounted on the cabin roof back of the pilothouse.

She was hitched to the stern of a funny-lookin' barge, maybe twice as long as a wood flat, with a low-slung cabin runnin' the full length and a crackerbox upper deck at the stern end. She had gingerbread all over and a big sign on the roof which read *New Floating Palace.* Propped up against the stageplank was a big piece of slate with "SHOWBOAT TONIGHT" painted at the top. Underneath is said "Dr. Leonidas Pettibone presents:" Lettered in chalk below was "Robin Hood of Sherwood Forest—Admission 25 and 15 cents."

When I got back to the *Jessie Bill*, Fatback hustled me up a cup of coffee and some bread and cold gravy after I agreed to tell him what I'd seen. Then I put on a clean shirt and dug around in my bunk until I found my money bag. By half past seven, every-body was bunched up on the forecastle and the whole place stunk of bay rum and hair tonic. Bush McDonald wasn't in sight and I hoped that meant he had the watch. When a man goes ashore with the idea of havin' a good time, it's better if Bush ain't along.

When we got aboard, it was plain to see the *New Floating Palace* wasn't very new and wasn't much of a palace. She was floating and that's about all you could say and stay with the truth. There was a wire cage at the head of the plank with a runt of a guy inside selling tickets. Above his head was a sign which read "PATRONS WITH FIREARMS, KNIVES AND MISSILES WILL NOT BE ADMITTED."

The stage extended across the stern, maybe three feet above the deck. There was a raised catwalk along both bulkheads and the chairs there cost extra. Oil lamps were spaced about four feet apart on the bulkheads and there was a row of overhead lamps along the center aisle.

Our crew spread out over the first row of benches and we had a good view of everything, includin' the orchestra when they came out from behind the curtain and took their seats in front of the stage. I don't know how many people it takes to make an orchestra, but there was only four in this one: violin, cornet, banjo and snare drums. The drummer was a roly-poly fellow and I guess he counted for more than one because he was handy with the tambourine and once in a while he'd cut loose with a mouth organ, which was mounted around his neck on a wire and didn't take no hands.

But mostly I kept my eyes on the violin player, and I think everybody else did, too. She was no bigger'n a minute and about the prettiest girl I'd ever seen. Her hair was the color of new straw and it covered part of her face as she played. Then the cornet player stood up and blew a bunch of sour notes and that started the curtain moving. It squeaked and quivered for a while and finally somebody reached around from the other side and jerked it the rest of the way.

There in the middle of the stage was Robin Hood and Little John and Friar Tuck sittin' around what was supposed to be a campfire. There was a couple of trees close by and Little John was holding on to one to keep it from fallin' over. There was a big bunch of trees painted on the backdrop and up in one corner was some blue water and a faraway castle. It might have looked better if we hadn't been so close.

Robin Hood did most of the talkin'. He was wearing green tights and a green jacket that was a little snug—mostly around the middle. His eyes bugged out like his collar was too tight and he wore a pointed cap with a big red feather stuck in it. His hair hung down to his shoulders in the back and he had a spade beard that made me think of a picture of the devil I'd seen once at Sunday school.

He kept shouting about the poor people and how cruel the Sheriff of Nottingham was and how he tortured Robin Hood's men whenever he caught one. Near the end of the first act the sheriff's men was supposed to be over in the edge of the forest and there was a lot of racket offstage and some firecrackers to sound like gunfire. Robin and his boys dropped down on the ground and whipped out their bows and started shootin' back. They was usin' real arrows, too, because I could hear them thump when they hit the bulkhead.

Things got better in the second act when Maid Marian and her lady-in-waiting—that's what Cleve called her, anyway—showed up. I didn't give Maid Marian a second look, not when I saw her lady-in-waiting was the same girl with the violin. This time she had on a dress that looked like a couple of gunny sacks with holes cut in 'em, but it didn't make her any less pretty—not with those blue eyes and that yellow hair.

Robin Hood, he couldn't see anybody but Marian. He dropped down on one knee and kissed her hand all the way up to her elbow. He told her he was loyal to his majesty, the king, and he swore he never robbed anybody except a lot of crooked lords who hated the king. About that time the cornet player dished up some more sour notes and Marian threw up her hands and said her father would drive her out of the family castle if the sheriff's men found her here. Then she fainted dead away and Robin caught her just as the curtain closed.

The orchestra played a couple of tunes and the ticket-taker showed up with a box full of bottles which he said was his Famous Elixir. He had a voice like a frog and he kept goin' up and down the aisle tellin' how the stuff would cure about every ailment known to man. He also had a special price just for tonight, only 50 cents a bottle. I guess everybody was pretty healthy, because he didn't sell but a few bottles.

In the third act, things got worse for ol' Robin. There he was in prison with the sheriff snarling at him and askin' him whether he wanted to be hanged at sundown or sunup. The sheriff looked surprised when Maid Marian arrived and started beggin' for Robin's life. That rattled the sheriff some and he tried to kiss Marian but she kept dodgin' him. Then he announced he'd turn Robin loose providing he could pass a little test with his bow and arrow.

It was some test, let me tell you. The sheriff all of a sudden grabs the lady-in-waiting and pushes her up against a tree and pops a potato on her head. Then he lets Robin out of his cell, hands him his bow and quiver, and tells him to fire away. Marian screamed and carried on, but Robin said he could do it. He threaded up an arrow and rared back with Miss Gunny Sack standin' there never battin' an eye. Then he eased off and got out another arrow. He did that maybe three times and by then I could hardly stand it. The whole place was as quiet as an undertakin' parlor. I wasn't even breathin' when the arrow flashed and two pieces of potato hit the deck—just like that. I never would've believed it if I hadn't seen it. I don't remember what happened after that, but when the curtain swung shut, we all stood up and whistled and clapped. We didn't stop either, and Robin and all the rest kept comin' back, smilin' and bowin'.

We was startin' to leave when Robin Hood came out on the stage by himself and told us what a fine audience we were and asked us where we was from. Then he pulled off his cap and all his long hair came with it. Up close, he looked a lot older. He was as bald as an eggplant and the sweat was drippin' off his beard.

"I am Dr. Leonidas Pettibone," he announced, "the foremost impresario of London and Paris and a member of the faculty of the Royal Academy of Arts." It was somethin' to hear, the way the words rolled off his tongue—like a big city preacher. There was more, but I didn't know half the words.

Then he dropped down on a bench and his head sagged down on his chest like all the air had been let out of him. I suppose it was the strain of splittin' that potato. Some of the crew started askin' questions, but he held up his hand for silence.

"Gentlemen, I must solicit your help," he said and this time he wasn't half so pompous. "You are the first decent souls we have encountered since our ill-fated departure from St. Louis." To hear him tell it, there was nothin' but cutthroats on one side of the river and savages on the other.

It wasn't long until we was all feelin' sorry for him, what with all the trouble they'd had. They was robbed of more'n $100 in Hannibal and Little John and Friar Tuck got tossed in jail on some trumped-up charges in Quincy. Their showboat sprung a leak below Canton and it took the most part of a week to put her back in shape. Then the *Prairie Flower* started havin' engine trouble around Keokuk and like he said, it had been one damned thing after another ever since.

Now the *Prairie Flower*'s dead in the water with a busted crankshaft. "We've been sitting here for ten days slowly starving to death," the doctor moaned. "Never have I seen so many rude bumpkins in one community. Those who patronize us come only to heap ridicule upon our cultural efforts. And the preachers, even they oppose us. But do they oppose the saloons? Of course not! Let me tell you, friends, this place is a sinkhole of iniquity!"

Right then I knew Read's Landing was a lot worse place than I thought. When the doctor slowed down a little, Four-Mile asked him how he got hooked up with Cap'n Joe Hartley and the

Prairie Flower. That set him off again. "That man has done nothing but bleed me! What possessed me to hire him and his boat for
the season, I'll never know. He found a worthless calliope and
charged me three times what it was worth. Half of the keys won't
even play."

For a minute I thought he was gonna cry. But he got hold of
himself and when he found out who our captain was, he began to
work on ol' Lafe with a proposition to tow the showboat to Fort
Snelling. But Lafe didn't want any part of it. In fact, he put on
almost as good a show as Dr. Pettibone, tellin' him that some big
lumberman was waitin' for the *Jessie Bill* at Stillwater and how
much money was at stake.

I was all for helpin' those poor people and I was glad when
the fog kept us tied up the next morning. Sometime in the
forenoon Four-Mile and Cleve went up the bank and when they
came back, both of them was upset. The way Cleve told it, they
stopped in one of the saloons just to see how bad it was and there
was a bunch of loggers laughin' and carryin' on about how they
was gonna take over the showboat this very night. The only thing
they was quarreling about was whether to sink it or burn it.

When Pot Belly heard about it, he allowed he'd take a look at
the *Prairie Flower* and see what he could do in the way of
repairs. Mudcat went with him and in about an hour they was
back. I could hear Pot Belly cussin' as he came up the plank. "A
boar's nest, that's what that engine room is! There's more things
wrong with that boat than any human being could ever fix."

The fog was liftin' some and Wabasha Dan was ready to head
up into Lake Pepin. But Four-Mile put his foot down and said we
weren't goin' nowhere, not until those loggers settled down or
we figured out a way to patch up the *Prairie Flower.* Dan and the
captain didn't like it, but both of them knew better than to cross
Four-Mile when he's got his back up.

I was sure Four-Mile had some kind of a scheme in the back
of his head and when he and Cleve headed for the showboat in
the middle of the afternoon, I tagged along. They didn't tell Dr.
Pettibone what they'd heard in the saloon, but they said the crew
of the *Jessie Bill* would sit down in front tonight, just so there
wouldn't be any trouble. Pettibone said he'd let us all in free and

he was so grateful he gave each of us a bottle of his Famous Elixir. I was scared Four-Mile might want me to taste it, but he just sniffed the stuff and said a man ought to be mighty sick before he tried it.

The doctor herded us up to the top deck where the players and musicians were havin' an early supper. It was slim pickin', let me tell you. We shook hands all-around and I could tell I was blushin' when I met the lady-in-waiting. She did a little curtsy which was about as graceful as anything I'd ever seen. Her name was Amy and Maid Marian, her sister, went by Clara.

Pettibone explained that they was his step-daughters. He called their mother Dame May and he told us she was from Philadelphia and a kin of Benjamin Franklin. And was I surprised when I found out she played the part of the Sheriff of Nottingham! She wore a sour face and when she shook hands, she had a grip like a roustabout.

There were four others in the company and all of 'em looked underfed except Dame May and Archie, the ticket-taker and medicine man. Little John was the drummer and Friar Tuck was the cornet player and there was a tall fellow with mutton chop whiskers called Duke who played the banjo and the calliope.

I could feel trouble in my bones when we went aboard the *New Floating Palace* a little before seven. Four-Mile led the way and we filled up the front bench except for Cleve and Limber Jim who stood by the ticket cage outside. There was a lot of noise on the levee and it wasn't long until the whole cabin was full, including those high-priced seats along the bulkheads. They was passin' bottles back and forth and the whole place stunk of booze and sweat. Pretty soon everybody started stompin' their feet and clappin' in rhythm and when the orchestra finally came out and started to play, you could hardly hear the music for all the catcalls. Right then I knew this was no place for Amy and her violin, and no place for a peace-lovin' mud clerk, either.

The curtain hadn't been open for more'n a minute or two when somebody hit Little John in the chest with an egg. Quick as a flash, Robin Hood threaded up his bow and stepped to the edge of the stage with a steel-tipped arrow pulled back as far as it would go. He just stood there, pointing it at the crowd.

Everybody got back in their seats and the whole place was dead quiet.

"We will proceed with the play," he announced and his voice was strong and full of scorn. But he hadn't hardly turned around when the eggs started flyin' like snowballs. The two girls began to scream and then some roughneck heaved a chair from the starboard side of the cabin and flattened Friar Tuck. Little John threw it back as hard as he could and the whole crowd rose up with a howl and headed for the stage. About the best our crew could do was slow 'em down. At first all I could see was feet and that was because I was under a bench. Somebody got the curtain closed but a dozen or so hands reached out and the whole thing came down with a crash and a cloud of dust. Out of the corner of my eye I saw Cleve pushin' the showboat people out the stern door at the back of the stage, all except Doc Pettibone who was swinging his fists and not hittin' much.

That door looked good to me, too, and when I finally worked my way around to it, I saw Four-Mile grab ol' Robin Hood and tell him to get all his folks on the *Jessie Bill* as fast as he could. We was losin' ground fast until Four-Mile yelled somethin' at Pinhead Grant and pointed across the stage. Each grabbed one end of the curtain and together they gave a mighty heave. In one swoop, they took the feet right out from under about ten of those cutthroats and dumped 'em in the orchestra section in a tangle of arms and legs. It was beautiful! That gave us a little time and we beat a fast retreat, first to the *Prairie Flower* and then down the levee to the *Jessie Bill*, with those loggers nippin' at our heels like a pack of wolves.

Pot Belly had steam up, but I couldn't see how we was going to get away from the landing without that whole mob coming aboard. Ercel Waters discouraged them some by swinging a five-foot piece of chain while Argonaut Smith cut the mooring lines with an axe. I don't mind admittin' I was scared. Somehow, Grumble Jones got the stageplank up and we backed out, catchin' a shower of rocks and whisky bottles and I don't know what all.

Let me tell you, those crazy loggers was on a tear. They wanted blood and by now I don't think it mattered much whose it was. They was swarmin' over the showboat and the *Prairie*

Flower both and it was plain to me that the *New Floating Palace* was never gonna survive that kind of treatment. Only I forgot about Limber Jim Gray, the best gunner in Sherman's Army. Orange fire belched from the *Jessie Bill*'s front end and there was a big roar that made me grab my ears. As soon as I crawled out of my hidin' place in the deckhouse, I saw the mountain howitzer, weighted down with flour sacks and firewood. The smoke smelled awful and right in the thick of it was Limber Jim, whoopin' and shakin' his fist.

We wasn't more'n 50 feet or so off the landing and when the big gun roared again, it took all the fight out of that mob. They were fallin' all over each other and the scramble got so bad that a bunch fell in the river. Women was screamin' and horses was jumpin' and squealin' at the hitching rail above the landing. There was hardly a soul in sight when we cut the showboat loose from the *Prairie Flower* and took it in tow. As soon as we headed up river, everybody crowded around Limber Jim, shakin' his hand and poundin' him over the back. Bush McDonald's eyes was about the size of saucers. "How many did you kill?" he demanded.

Limber Jim slapped his leg. "I didn't kill none, boy. Not a one. I didn't have no shells. Those was just powder charges. Nothin' else."

Ol' Pettibone dug a medal out of his trunk and pinned it on Jim's shirt. And that wasn't all. Dame May pushed him up against the bulkhead and gave him a kiss—square on the mouth. When he recovered, Jim allowed that any artilleryman worth his salt would have done what he done. He loved every minute of it when he told how he and Argonaut decided to dig the howitzer out of the woodpile when it looked like there was gonna be big trouble.

"Just tell me one thing," Four-Mile said. "Where'd you get the powder?"

"Oh, I bought myself a keg in Fort Madison," Limber Jim replied. "What's the sense of havin' the only mountain howitzer on the river if you can't fire it?"

Chapter Nine

If I thought boiler explosions a mystery,
I could not have slept so comfortably
over them for fifty years.
—Capt. Walter A. Blair

MAY 28, 1880:

When it comes to seeing the funny side of things, there's nobody better'n Cleve Allen. He's good at mockin' people, too, and it wasn't long until he had Doc Pettibone and the captain down pat. "The Steamer *Jessie Bill* presents Leonidas and Lafayette," he would say, draggin' out each name while makin' all kinds of funny faces. He'd talk and walk like one, then he'd throw in a little dance and make like he was the other. Laugh, I laughed until my sides ached.

"England's greatest actor and America's richest lumber baron," he called them. "There may be bigger liars in this world," he said with a straight face, "but I'll bet you couldn't find a pair that can lie with more class."

The two of them spent a good part of the night talkin' after we left Read's Landing. Talkin' and drinkin' the captain's red wine, that is. We raised Red Wing about half past nine the next morning and as soon as we tied up, the captain asked all hands to come to a meetin' on the forecastle. All the showboat folks was there, too. With great fanfare, Lafe announced that the crew of the *Jessie Bill* had been invited to join the *New Floating Palace* company in two benefit performances of "Robin Hood," one tonight and one tomorrow night. How he laid it on. "This could be a first in showboat history," he said, "the skillful blending of professional and amateur."

Then he explained this was Doc Pettibone's way of showing his appreciation to us *Jessie Bill* people for our fearless efforts at Read's Landing. And he also pointed out the money will help those poor troupers get back on their feet. Mostly, when the captain comes up with a new idea, all he gets are growls. But this time everybody whistled and cheered. Well, almost everybody. Four-Mile and Wabasha Dan weren't what you'd call excited, but they didn't have anything bad to say. I couldn't believe it.

Ol' Pettibone took charge and I never saw so much activity. Leastwise, not on the *Jessie Bill*. There was Pot Belly, offering his services to the orchestra. He produced a harmonica from somewhere and when he whipped through a stanza of "Marching Through Georgia" everybody clapped. He had an ocarina, too, which he loaned to Grumble Jones. Pinhead Grant was shy about it, but he owned up that he had a fiddle in the bottom of his chest and it was plain he was ready to play with only a small amount of coaxin'.

I could tell the captain wasn't gonna be satisfied unless he got some big part in the show. Right off he told Pettibone how he used to perform back in his school days and it was finally agreed that he would play the Sheriff of Nottingham. Dame May didn't want to be left out, so Pettibone said she could take over as Maid Marian. Now Clara is no beauty, but it seemed to me that they lost a lot in that swap.

For a minute, I had a strong notion to try out as one of the sheriff's men. But I soon saw that everybody and his dog wanted to be a sheriff's man—Mudcat, Limber Jim, even Bushel Butt. Ol' Pettibone asked me to take care of the curtain, forgettin' for the moment that the *New Floating Palace* didn't have a curtain. I was disappointed until Amy gave me one of her smiles and said she'd help me get the curtain back on the track. It was a cobbled-up job, but I got it so it'd work if you didn't pull too hard. I don't mind admittin' I took my time. Who wouldn't with a pretty gal like Amy to help?

Not havin' a calliope, Doc Pettibone said we'd have to hustle or we'd never get a crowd. Archie hitched on his sandwich board with big letters tellin' all about the show, front and back. Dame May said he needed a little help, so Friar Tuck tuned up his cornet and the two of them went marchin' up the levee.

Dame May and the girls whipped together another "Robin Hood" sign using a piece of plank and some paint. They put rope handles on it and hung it between the two ugliest men on the boat, Bush and Argonaut. Then Pettibone got Little John and his drum and sent the three of them off in the opposite direction, scarin' the daylights out of every child and chicken in sight.

Maybe it was because the weather was good. Or maybe it was because the people of Red Wing were hungry for some entertainment. Anyway, they came flockin' in and Archie got so far behind in the ticket cage that Cleve had to help out. The place was full and runnin' over by 10 minutes after seven and the orchestra came out early to keep the crowd from gettin' too restless. They didn't sound so good with all those new members, but they were loud and the folks out front seemed to like 'em. I had a few bad moments with that awful curtain, but at least it didn't fall down. The first act went off mainly without a hitch. I could tell ol' Lafe was doin' his best as the Sheriff of Nottingham, but he never would have made it if those people hadn't whispered to him and pointed him where he was supposed to go. The crowd didn't know the difference. They was all havin' a good time, clappin' and cheerin' for no reason at all. And when it came time for Archie to give his medicine spiel at intermission, people were pushin' and shovin' to get rid of their money.

There was a few rough spots in the last act but it didn't matter because by that time ol' Pettibone had the whole place right in his hip pocket. When the crowd figured out he might be going to shoot a potato off Amy's head, they couldn't hardly stand it. Neither could I, to tell the truth. They kept callin' "No! no!" and when Robin Hood pulled back his bow for about the fifth time, the place was dead quiet just like always.

Then the arrow flashed, the potato fell to the deck in two pieces and the crowd sort of exploded. They hardly stopped clappin' for 10 minutes. Ol' Pettibone grabbed Amy by the hand and he did a bow and she made a little curtsy and they had to do it four or five more times before they got things goin' again. I was lovin' every minute of it and I suppose that's why I forgot to pull the curtain at the end. Dame May reached around and poked me and I pulled too hard and about half the blamed thing fell down. But nobody seemed to notice. The crowd was cheerin' again and all the actors came out on the stage, including the captain who kept tryin' to muscle his way up front. I was watchin' Amy and I smiled when I thought how much work it was gonna take to get that curtain back in shape.

By noon the next day, it was plain the captain would never be the same again. There he was up on the roof, practicin' his lines and jumpin' around like a sword-fighter. He had rigged up a new costume, including a big hat with a plume. I don't think I ever saw a funnier get-up. A little later he and Doc Pettibone had their heads together up on the levee where nobody could hear and Cleve Allen said they had been meetin' like that off'n on most of the day.

I knew I'd be sorry, but my curiosity had the best of me, so I went down to the engine room and asked Pot Belly what was goin' on. He took a deep breath and the words came rollin' out. "Clapsaddle is off his rocker for sure this time!" he declared. "He's gone on this actin' business, gone I tell you. You should've heard him. He thinks he's a natural-born actor and he wants to spend the rest of his life on the stage. Why any fool knows he'd starve to death in less'n a month."

I don't remember half the stuff he said, but he got my attention quick when he began to rave about the captain's deal with Doc Pettibone. Right off he warned me that I needn't have any doubts. "It's the gospel, I got it straight from the captain hisself. He and Pettibone have already shook on it, except for a few little details here and there. What do you think of that? We'll push the *New Floating Palace* up and down the river, puttin' on at least four shows a week. Pettibone will give the captain one-third interest in the showboat. He'll also guarantee Lafe a good part in every play and second billing right behind Pettibone hisself."

Believe me, that was enough to make my head spin. "Does Four-Mile know about this?" I asked. "And Wabasha Dan?"

"Oh, you bet they do," Pot Belly said, shakin' a finger in my face. "Haven't you heard Dan carryin' on up in the pilothouse? I've never seen him so hot under the collar. He said he was havin' no part of a showboat and he called Pettibone and his people a bunch of swindlers. And worse.

"Four-Mile was pretty worked up at first, but then he calmed down some and told Dan to do the same. Dan was chewin' on his cigar somethin' fierce and he said he was gettin' off the boat just as soon as he could get his gear together. But Four-Mile made him promise he'd wait at least one more day."

Pot Belly was still talkin' a blue streak when I eased out the engine room door.

The day wasn't turning out too good, mainly because Amy was busy doin' somethin' and I had to fix that cussed curtain by myself. I hardly had time to get a little supper before people started linin' up in front of the ticket cage. Those Red Wingers really like their showboats, let me tell you. The place was packed again, includin' some folks who were back for the second night.

Right off, the orchestra sounded 100 percent better. They even had a little solo part for Pot Belly's harmonica, and when he stood up and did a chorus of "Pretty Red Wing," how they did cheer! The first act started off good enough, but the first time the Sheriff of Nottingham appeared, there was something that told me ol' Lafe was gonna get himself in trouble. You talk about a show-off! Whatever he did, he tried to hog the stage and a couple of times it go so bad the crowd whistled at him. I could tell Doc Pettibone was gettin' irritated and once he stomped on the captain's foot. Lafe let out a low holler and Robin Hood pretended like it was an accident.

Sales of the Famous Elixir were even better'n the night before and the bow-and-arrow scene was a whoppin' big success. The last act was well along and everything was runnin' smooth when Lafe had to go and pull a whizzer. And I mean a whizzer! He didn't have much to say right then and he was supposed to be back out of the road. Of course he wasn't. Maid Marian backed into him, on purpose I think, and then she bent over just a little to say something to her lady-in-waiting. I don't know what made Lafe do it, but quick as a wink, he gave her a pinch. Right on her rear end. There was fire in her eye and she turned around slow like, not speakin' her lines or anything. By now, Lafe knew he was in big trouble and he started backin' away. They was both movin' in a slow circle when Dame May let him have it. If it had been a righthand punch, he might have seen it. But this one came from the left, a looping blow that took him square on the hose. Lafe's head snapped and he tumbled backwards off the stage, smashin' Little John's drum to smithereens.

I reckon the crowd thought it was all part of the show. Anyway, you could tell they loved it the way they yelled and stomped. By now ol' Pettibone had his dander up and he grabbed the curtain rope and gave it a mighty pull. The whole mess came crashin' down and a piece of the track smacked him on the head. That was almost more'n he could take. He marched to the center of the stage and spat out the words: "The show is over!" Then he marched off, trembling with rage.

Chapter Ten

> *The moth-eaten fiction about whisky as a cure*
> *for snake-bites was everywhere viewed as*
> *gospel and widely availed of—cure and pre-*
> *ventive. There used to be a man on the upper*
> *river known as Rattlesnake Jake, who had been*
> *bitten and rescued so many times he had*
> *become famous, and was dead before it was*
> *discovered that the marks on his leg had been*
> *made with a brad-awl.*
> —Charles Edward Russell

JUNE 9, 1880:

There's a lot of rivers in this world I've never seen, but I don't suppose I'll ever find one half as pretty as the St. Croix. She runs clear and clean from Stillwater, Minn., to Prescott, Wis., where she empties into the Mississippi, about 25 miles, give or take a little. Oh, there's more to her than that, but the boats don't run above Stillwater because of the catch-booms where the logs come down from the streams above. Some folks say this stretch is really a lake and not a river, but whatever you call it, it's a thing of beauty. The sandbars are golden and the meadows along the bank are extra green. There are high rock bluffs that climb straight out of the water and big stands of hardwood, pine and birch. There's also a lot of peace and quiet on the St. Croix, and that includes the *Jessie Bill*, too. After Read's Landing and Red

Wing, we could use plenty of both. In case you're wonderin', I'm happy to say we're out of the showboat business and back in the raftin' business. Thank the Lord. This morning Wabasha Dan was hummin' a little tune up in the pilothouse and that's a mighty rare event. And Four-Mile was wearin' a kind of half smile and pattin' his rousters on the back. That's rarer still.

In fact, everybody's feelin' great, except Cap'n Lafe, of course. We haven't hardly seen him since we parted company with the *New Floating Palace*. And that's fine, because with a busted nose, he's not too good to look at.

Doc Pettibone came lookin' for him right after the show Saturday night, but Lafe locked himself in his cabin and wouldn't come out. Pettibone was back early Sunday morning and when he still couldn't raise the captain, he asked to speak with Four-Mile, makin' sure he was close enough to Lafe's door to be heard inside.

"Mr. Freeman, on behalf of the theatrical company of the *New Floating Palace*, I wish it publicly known that all oral agreements reached with Captain Lafayette Clapsaddle are hereby abrogated."

Four-Mile didn't say a word, probably because he didn't know whether bein' abrogated was good or bad.

With hardly a pause, Pettibone continued. "It is also my solemn duty to reprimand said Clapsaddle for conduct unbecoming a thespian and I ask you to inform him that I am taking formal steps to forever bar him from the theatre, both here and abroad.

"While we of the *New Floating Palace* appreciate the invaluable assistance rendered by you, Mr. Freeman, and your associates, we feel that it is in the best interest of all that we part company at the next town."

Four-Mile didn't answer right off. Instead he rubbed his chin slow-like and it looked to me like he was tryin' to keep a smile off his face. "Partin' company is the best idea you've had yet, doctor, and we'll oblige you just as soon as we can tie you off at Prescott. Shouldn't be more'n an hour or so. That'll give me and you plenty of time to settle up."

Ol' Pettibone flinched like he was shot. "I beg pardon?"

"Settle up," Four-Mile boomed. "I've got a bill here and I know you'd have trouble sleepin' if you left us and forget to meet all your financial obligations."

With that, Four-Mile produced a crumpled piece of paper and unfolded it with great deliberation. "Towing, Red Wing to Prescott," he read. "We ain't there yet, you understand, 20 miles at $2.50 per mile, $50, a real bargain. Miscellaneous expenses, including vittles for the *New Floating Palace,* and a small amount of gunpowder, $30.

"Least but not last, there's the *Jessie Bill*'s share of the ticket receipts, two performances, mind you. If we was greedy, we'd ask for half, but since we was all beginners, so to speak, we'll be happy to settle for a third. We know the ticket count is accurate because Mr. Allen here got the figures from your man, Archie. Just to show you how fair we are, we're askin' nothing for pain and suffering received while protecting you folks from that mob at Read's Landing. Furthermore, since Captain Clapsaddle was something less than a gentleman during Saturday's performance, we will discount the bill by $25, leaving a sum of $410 due and payable."

Pettibone's eyes flashed and his face turned a terrible shade of red. Then the air sort of went out of him and he opened his carpetbag and slowly dug out his purse, not sayin' a word.

We left the channel at the foot of Prescott Island and eased the *New Floating Palace* into the Wisconsin bank a few rods below the Prescott landing. Argonaut and Pinhead got her snubbed in nicely and by a little after nine, we were ready to drop our bow lines and head up the St. Croix. There was talk that Pinhead was gonna stay with the showboat and that didn't surprise me none because I knew he was sweet on Clara.

Here it was time to say goodbye and nobody seemed to know how to do it. People were standin' around in little bunches and for no reason at all, the place got awful quiet. Then Pinhead showed up with his bedroll and right off Four-Mile demanded to know where he thought he was goin'.

"Tell the cap'n I'm quittin'," Pinhead replied and there was a sheepish look on his face.

"There's no quittin' to it," Four-Mile roared. "You're a deserter and you're fired!"

You can bet Pinhead didn't linger, but he no more'n got his feet planted on the showboat when Doc Pettibone appeared in the door and pushed him back. Then the two of them marched straight for Four-Mile.

"Sir, I believe we have a little more settling up to do," Pettibone said with a smirk.

"What're you tryin' to pull?" Four-Mile wanted to know.

"Did you fire this man? On what grounds?" Pettibone demanded.

"For desertion," Four-Mile said and the way he was gettin' worked up, I could tell Pinhead wished he was 10 miles down the river.

But ol' Pettibone kept borin' in. "The law says when you fire a man, you must pay him off on the spot. Mr. Grant here tells me he has not been paid since Fort Madison, and then only partially. You owe him $27 and he has authorized me to collect it. If you do not pay him here and now, I assure you the sheriff will be waiting when you return downriver."

Four-Mile was steamin', let me tell you, but when he eyed Pettibone standin' there was his arms folded and his jaw stickin' out, he knew the shoe was on the other foot and he was beat. Oh, it pained him, but he got out his money and counted it out in Doc's hand.

It didn't take us long to find out that the St. Croix was a lot busier place than we thought. We met our first raft comin' down about seven miles above Prescott near the mouth of the Kinnickinnic River. There was several brails tied along the bank at Black Bass Bar and when we got to St. Mary's Point, we had to shave the bank pretty close to keep out of the road of the *LaCrosse Lady,* pushin' one of the biggest lumber rafts I've ever seen. No logs, mind you, but dimension stuff, already cut. I don't know much about lumber rafts, but they build them in what they call cribs. This one was 20 cribs long and six wide. Cleve got out his pencil and paper and figured it was 640 feet long and 100 feet wide. Whew!

Stillwater is a lively town, too lively, if you ask me. The streets was bankful with loggers who had just come down on a big drive and I gave 'em a wide berth whenever I could. The catch-booms are located at Lookout Point and the raftin' works stretch out from there right to the edge of town.

By now the captain was back in circulation and his nose looked halfway decent. He met some crony as soon as we tied up and he came back aboard all fired up, sayin' there was lots of rafts ready to go and not enough boats to move 'em. Usually you can figure most of what the captain brings back is misinformation, but not this time.

We'd hardly finished breakfast when some agent from the Musser Mill at Muscatine came aboard and offered us a raft. The captain dickered around for a while and he finally had the good sense to get Four-Mile in on the talks. They pushed pretty hard for a cash advance, but the agent said that was too big a risk with an ol' tub like the *Jessie Bill*. That put the captain in a big huff and he said he was through doin' business with the Mussers. But Four-Mile got him quieted down and the agent offered us $125 a string with a bonus of $200 if we could make delivery in nine days.

He wanted us on our way no later'n noon Tuesday and that gave us precious little time to lay in provisions, pick up a raft and get it in shape to run. Thanks to our showboat friends, there was cash for grub and a bunch of canthooks and some check line which Four-Mile said we had to have.

It rained all night and part of the morning, but we got the first piece on the buttin' block by ten o'clock. The second piece went faster and by late afternoon we raised Bayport, about four miles below Stillwater. Four-Mile kept crabbin' about the way the raft was framed and he made us travel on a slow bell until we redone some of the lines. Then he gave Wabasha Dan the high sign and I could feel the pitmans pick up the pace. I shut my eyes, and just for a minute, it was like we was standin' down the river on a brand-new boat.

It was almost dark when we hit the Mississippi and Wabasha Dan blew a whistle for the *New Floating Palace*. A few people waved from the stern, but try as I might, I couldn't see Amy. Then I had a terrible thought that kept me awake half the night: What if ol' Pettibone was a little low the next time he shot that potato off Amy's head?

When things go smooth for a whole day on the *Jessie Bill*, I start gettin' a little nervous. The river was rising and we made Smith's Landing before daybreak. In no time at all we raised Red Wing and by nine o'clock or so, we was over Sawdust Bar and into Lake Pepin. It's not really a lake, you understand, it just looks like one. Don't ask me why it's so wide, up to four miles in some places.

Anyway, the sky took on a sickly green color and all of a sudden the air was very still and very hot. Cleve said we should have tied up at Bay City, but it was too late for that. There wasn't time to get scared because Four-Mile had everybody out on the raft checkin' lines. He waved us all back when the wind started to blow something fierce and for a minute or two, I didn't think I was gonna make it.

All the while I could see a middlin'-sized boat comin' upstream and she was poppin' around like a cork. There's a joke about people gettin' sea-sick on Lake Pepin, but I don't think it's so funny. Because it's so wide, it's also shallow in most places and that makes the waves higher'n meaner than any spot on the river.

First the wind came in gusts. Then the rain started and the wind got stronger'n stronger until a body could hardly stand up. The sky went from green to black and with the rain comin' in sheets, you couldn't see your hand in front of your face. I've heard people talk about Lake Pepin storms all my life, but I didn't know they could get this bad. I know the waves was higher'n my head. When the head of the raft began to swing, there was no way Wabasha Dan could keep us on course.

In no time at all we was crossways in the river and maybe that's what saved us because it put our stern to the wind. The raft was pitchin' and rollin' something awful and I kept thinkin' the lines would start poppin' any minute. We was already takin' water and it was plain that if we ever came loose from the raft, we'd capsize for sure. Right about then the biggest wave of all hit us and the whole raft shuddered and shook like a dyin' thing. It wasn't long 'til the wind and rain began to slack off and we couldn't believe what we was seein'. You probably won't believe it either. Remember that boat we was meetin'? She'd of sunk for sure, except that last big wave picked her up and set her on the front starboard corner of the raft. So help me, that's the truth! It busted up one brail and part of another. But with the storm over, it didn't take too long to round up the logs and get 'em framed back in shape.

The boat turned out to be the *Elizabeth Ann,* a little rafter from Savannah which had seen better days. Let me tell you, her crew was mighty happy to help us get our raft back together. I figured there was two things that saved us and the *Elizabeth Ann,* too: My prayers and Four-Mile's snug lines.

I was hopin' we'd pass Read's Landing during the night, in view of what happened on our last visit. But it didn't work out that way and the sun was a couple of hours high when we raised the town at the foot of the lake. There were several rafters tied up at the landing, but the only thing stirrin' was a yawl with an oarsman and a pudgy fellow wearin' a beaver hat sittin' in the bow. It looked like they was headed across the river and I thought to myself they'd better hustle. Instead, the guy on the oars quit rowin' and Mr. Beaver Hat stood up and started wavin' his arms. Nobody in his right mind tries to hail a boat with a raft in tow. You don't need to be half smart to know that stoppin' a raft takes a lot of doin' and at least a mile of river.

Wabasha Dan gave the yawl a big blast on the whistle and the oarsman started pullin' for dear life. Another few seconds and we'd a run right over 'em. The guy in the hat was still wavin' when we went by, yellin' something about the *Jessie Bill.* Maybe he didn't know what he was doin', but he knew what boat he wanted. The captain didn't say much, but he was nervous as a cat for the rest of the morning. Cleve said Mr. Beaver Hat was probably one of Lafe's many creditors, or else somebody wantin' to arrest us all for shootin' a cannon at the good folks of Read's Landing. Either way, it spelled trouble to me.

Sometime after noon we spotted a yawl behind us, but it was too far away to tell if it was the one we'd seen earlier. The captain kept the glasses on it as long as he could and twice he went to the pilothouse and asked Wabasha Dan to call for a little more steam.

We was low on fuel and Pot Belly told the captain we'd better put in at Dominick's woodyard below Minneiska unless we wanted to tie up and cut our own wood before morning. It was near dusk when we landed and we didn't have more'n a couple of cords on board when our roly-poly friend came along side in a skiff with two oarsmen. I figured he'd come overland to Minneiska and this time he wasn't gonna let us get away.

"Is this the steamer *Jessie Bill*?" he asked as he climbed up on the guard and dusted off his striped pants. Nobody answered, but that didn't slow him down. "Permit me to introduce myself," he said, grinnin' like a chessy cat. "I am Crawford C. Crabtree of Crabtree and Crowfoot, the oldest law firm in Cincinnati, Ohio."

If you've already guessed that Cap'n Lafe had gone into hiding, you're right. Four-Mile and Cleve walked out on the front end and the rest of us stood back in the shadows, nobody sayin' a word.

"Are you the master of this vessel, sir?" Crabtree asked, stickin' his hand out to Four-Mile.

Four-Mile didn't want any hand-shakin'. "The captain is ailin'. Just state your business, mister."

All at once our visitor looked a little scared. "Gentlemen, please," he said, makin' the peace sign with his palm. "I assure you I am not here to cause trouble. On the contrary, I am searching for a man who is believed to be a member of your crew and who is the heir to a large fortune."

Ol' Lafe has a good set of ears and I guess it was that word "fortune" that brought him out of his cabin on the double. Quick as a wink, he was down the ladder, pushin' people out of the way so he could get ahold of Crabtree's hand. He pumped it good, tellin' Crabtree how welcome he was and apologizin' for not bein' on hand to greet him. "Now, pray tell, who are you looking for, sir?" Lafe asked.

"An Englishman," Crabtree replied. "His name is Reginald Glendenning, late of Kingbridge, South Devon."

The captain looked blank. "There must be a mistake," he said. "We have no one aboard by that name."

"We have been searching for this man for more than a year and we are sure he is living under an assumed name," the lawyer said. "Actually, I know very little about him. He is fifty-five years of age and he came to this country with his mother and step-father, many years ago. If he is alive—and we are convinced he is—then he is the sole beneficiary of a vast estate that includes an earldom and at least two castles."

After that, Crabtee had people fallin' all over him and there was no way he could keep up with all the questions. By now it was almost dark and the captain sent me and Bush McDonald to break out some lanterns so our guest wouldn't trip and fall overboard.

I had just lit the first one when I heard a commotion back in the deckhouse. There was a mixture of loud laughter and angry words and then everything got quiet. Fatback sidestepped his way through the crowd, wipin' away the sweat with his apron tail. The light flickered across his face and he just stood there, movin' his lips but not makin' a sound. Then the words came and not one soul there was prepared for what he heard: "I reckon I'm the man you're lookin' for," he said.

Chapter Eleven

*The details of the river, once learned,
were so indelibly printed
on the mind of the pilot that it seemed
as though eyes were almost superfluous.*
—George Byron Merrick

JUNE 18, 1880:

Only on a crazy boat like the *Jessie Bill* would you find a cook named Reginald who's an earl and who owns two castles. I still can't believe it. And neither can anybody else, includin' Fatback. We keep askin' him about his family background, but mostly he plays it dumb. One thing I found out quick-like: he don't like to be called Reggie.

At first, it was pretty excitin' stuff, but after two weeks the whole thing sort of turned my stomach. Mostly, it's the captain's fault, the way he buttered up Fatback and insisted we call him Your Honor. I get mad, just thinkin' about it. Fatback never was easy to get along with and now he's ten times worse. I know because, sorry to say, I'm now the assistant cook in addition to all my other duties. The captain said Reginald was workin' too hard and needed some help. The job should have been Bush McDonald's, but like I told you, Fatback won't let him set foot in the galley. And that's not the half of it. Fatback's now bunkin' forward in the clerk's office and I'm stuck in that little cubbyhole off the kitchen. Boar's nest would be a better word for it. As soon as it quits rainin', I may move out on the raft where I can have a little privacy.

Just to bring you up to date, Lawyer Crabtree expected Fatback to go with him back to Ohio, but Cap'n Lafe wasn't about to let him get away. No, sir. So he kept tellin' Fatback how much we needed him and how it was his duty to stay on until we delivered the raft to Muscatine.

"For sure, we'll get him on the first train to Cincinnati," Lafe promised and Crabtree finally agreed. Then the lawyer took a big leather case out of his breast pocket and handed over a bunch of money to Fatback, for expenses I suppose. He also made Fatback sign a receipt. I never did hear how much he got, but Pot Belly said there was easy enough greenbacks to choke a billy goat. "Make that two billy goats," he said.

The next thing we knew, the captain had cooked up a big scheme to keep Fatback on the boat. "We're going to form a company of our own with Reginald as chairman of the board and me as president," I heard Lafe tell Cleve Allen. "We'll buy out two or three lumber companies and have our own fleet of boats."

The captain was wavin' his arms and talkin' in a loud voice like he always does when he's excited.

"What does Fatback say about this?" Cleve asked.

"Why, he's all for it," Lafe said. "In fact, he told me he had had a keen interest in business and commerce since childhood. When I first hired him, I knew he was a diamond in the rough. But he's also sensitive, very sensitive, and we all have a duty to protect him. I shudder to think what might happen to him back East. I say let his friends look after him right here on the boat while that lawyer looks after his property in Cincinnati."

I'd never been ashore at Muscatine before, but I decided it was a lucky town. The people at Musser's Mill didn't give us trouble and we collected the $200 bonus, less a little for the few logs we lost during the Lake Pepin storm. With hard money in his pocket, Cap'n Lafe was also in fine fettle. Not only that, but it was plain he was droolin' over those greenbacks in Fatback's pocket and all those he was sure was still to come. He asked me to go with him to the First National Bank and on the way he told me we were done pushin' rafts for other folks.

"As soon as we get back to Beef Slough, we're going to buy our own raft and eliminate the middle man," he said. I didn't get it all, but comin' from the captain, it sounded risky to me.

Back at the boat, Lafe got out his account book and had me pay all hands, back wages included. The shock was almost more'n people could stand; Ercel Waters got up and said he wanted to take back all those nasty names he called the captain. The next thing we knew Lafe was into one of his speeches and he laid it on pretty thick, tellin' us we was in on the ground floor of a new company that would make the Weyerhaeusers look like small potatoes. Nobody paid much attention, but we sat up and took notice when he announced that we'd lay over in Muscatine until tomorrow, as long as everybody promised to stay out of jail and be on board ready to go by daylight. It's just as well that the folks back home didn't hear all the whistlin' and clappin' for ol' Lafe because they never would've believed it.

The captain laid in a fresh supply of wine and he and Fatback spent the night at the Howard Hotel. I know Lafe wasn't too keen about that, but he was afraid to let Fatback out of his sight. Cleve said the captain talked Fatback into buyin' some new clothes, but he had an awful time gettin' him to take a bath before he put 'em on.

It's maybe 300 miles from Muscatine to Beef Slough and somewhere in between, Fatback started believin' all the things Lafe had been tellin' him. Mind you, here was a man who hardly ever spoke a word and now all of a sudden he's got an opinion about everything. Most of all, he likes to tell people just what it is they're doin' wrong. He said Pot Belly wasn't gettin' enough speed out of the engines and he told Four-Mile we should be pushin' bigger rafts. Then he started in on the captain and all his big talk about buyin' his own raft. "There ain't a lumber company in the world that would trust Lafe Clapsaddle any further than they could throw him," he declared. For once, we all agreed with him.

Lafe threatened to break up the company and for the next couple of days things was quiet because the president wasn't speakin' to the chairman of the board. But whatever you say about the captain, you have to admit he knows how to wheel and deal. And that's all he did from the time he set foot on the Beef

Slough landing. Mostly, I think he just wanted to show Fatback he could do it.

First he had a talk with the manager of the Mississippi River Logging Company and then he took Fatback, all decked out in his new duds, to meet the president and all the big-wigs. According to Cleve, they all laughed when the captain said he wanted to buy a raft, but when they heard the story of Reginald Glendenning, they got very serious. They also had a big surplus of logs, Cleve said, and that didn't hurt the captain's position none. The president said the goin' price for a six-brail raft was $10,000, but he was willing to cut that to $9,000. Between 'em, Lafe and Fatback came up with $1,000 and that was the only money that changed hands. Then the captain signed over the *Jessie Bill* and he and Fatback gave their personal notes to cover the rest. The whole deal was down in black and white by Thursday afternoon. Cleve laughed when he said Lafe had trouble rememberin' how many times he had mortgaged the boat. "That's what you call high finance, Peter," he said.

It was Four-Mile's turn next and when he told the company how he wanted the raft built, the manager said he'd call the whole thing off. But he finally gave in and we got the raft all trussed up and headed down river in record time. At least it was a record for the *Jessie Bill*.

The river was risin' and Wabasha Dan allowed it would be safe to take the Buffalo cutoff down the east side of Lost Island. Four-Mile wasn't so sure, but he went along, knowin' it could save us as much as three hours. We was maybe nine miles below Beef Slough when we left the channel and headed east into Robuck's Run, a little gap of water that puts you into Pomme de Terre Chute, about two miles above the town of Buffalo. We was clippin' right along with plenty of water when we came out from the backside of a scrubby little island and all of a sudden the whole slough was full of rafts. I mean big ones, little ones, all sizes. Wabasha Dan reversed his engines and swore when the head of our raft nosed through a bunch of loose logs and finally bumped to a stop.

Four-Mile, for one, had trouble believin' what he was seein'. "There ain't no way that can be a legitimate operation," he barked. "If them folks over there are pirates like I think they are, we're in for trouble."

There was a boat working about a half mile to starboard with four or five people out on a raft handling the lines. It was on the small side and Mudcat Lewis said it looked like the *Hudson Bay,* a boat that used to be over on the Illinois River. There was three or four ramshackle buildings on the west bank of the chute with two more boats tied up nearby, the *Golden Gate* and the *Hiram Price.*

Cleve said as far as he could tell, the only way out was through a sheer-boom hooked to the east bank. Any brails or pieces comin' through the chute had to stop here. "I ain't one bit surprised," Pot Belly said in a high voice. Whenever he got worked up, his voice went up about two notches. "Ever' place we go, people are talkin' about log thieves. They're stealin' 'em blind at Beef Slough and West Newton, too. And in broad daylight!" As for the captain, he was gettin' jumpier by the minute. "Who does Dan think he is, taking this chute?" he complained. "Why didn't he keep us in the main channel where we belong?"

Late in the afternoon, Four-Mile said it was time we was testin' the water. He put Limber Jim and Argonaut in the yawl and told 'em to go see how hard it would be to open the sheer-boom. But they never found out. Two rifle shots rang out when they got close and nobody had to tell 'em to turn around and skedaddle home.

As darkness approached, Four-Mile dug a rusty old rifle out of the rope locker and sent Ercel Waters out on the front end to stand guard. He didn't have to wait long. A dugout canoe pulled along side and when Ercel challenged it, the lone occupant struck a match and lit a lantern. "Put down that piece, boy," he ordered. "There are two men out there behind you and if you so much as point that thing at me, you're dead."

For once, Ercel didn't argue.

"Who are you and what do you want?" Four-Mile demanded.

The man wore jack boots and buckskin pants and what looked like a horse blanket made into a cape. He had a full beard and curly black hair that bulged out from under his hat. "First off, what boat is this?" he called.

"*Jessie Bill*," somebody replied.

"Well, *Jessie Bill*, you're gonna wish to hell you'd a stayed out of this here slough. We got a powerful lot of logs to move out of here tonight and we don't like strangers watchin' us. Not one bit."

"What ever you're doin' you won't get away with it for long," Pot Belly told him.

"Who says we can't?" Black Beard shot back. "Now you people listen and you listen careful. You can stay on this broken-down boat for now if you follow orders. If you don't, you just might get fed to the fish. Stay put and don't try no funny business. Remember, a boat like yours burns awful easy. At first light, I want you to drop your raft and leave the lines right where they are, you hear? Then we'll decide what to do with your boat. If'n somethin' happens to it, it sure wouldn't be no loss," he said with a big laugh. "Good night an' sweet dreams." Then he blew out the lantern and we could hear him paddlin' away.

I can tell you nobody did much sleepin' that night. Not those boats that was movin' logs through the sheer-boom and most of all not the folks on the *Jessie Bill*. Those that weren't standing guard was diggin' through the woodpile, pickin' out pieces of a certain size. They stripped off the bark and squared the ends, then they worked 'em with a rasp to make 'em round as they could and they greased 'em with lard.

Sometimes I ain't too smart and it didn't hit me what they was doin' until I saw Limber Jim Gray settin' up his mountain howitzer out on the front end. Man, that made my blood tingle! Jim called her his Fort Madison Sweetheart and he wrapped his arms around the barrel like it was a livin' thing. "Whatever comes out of that muzzle is travelin' 650 feet per second," he said proudly. "She can shoot the balls off a brass monkey at 900 yards."

We had steam up a little after dawn and as soon as it was good and light, we unhitched the raft. Cleve had the glasses on the *Hudson Bay*, the near boat, and when it looked like people was comin' aboard for breakfast, he said it was time to go. Somebody had to make a move pretty soon, and we figured we might as well be first.

Wabasha Dan backed away from the buttin' block and eased us slow-like along the string of rafts toward the pirate boat.

When we were 600 yards or so away, he put our nose up against a half-raft and what must be the first gunboat ever on the Upper Mississippi was ready for action. Just thinkin' about it made my heart pound.

Limber Jim had picked Mudcat Lewis and Argonaut Smith for his gun crew and they was all business. They had the howitzer lashed to the bow bitts with extra lines running to the port and starboard cavels so she wouldn't jump around. The carriage was weighted down with odd pieces of machinery and whatever they could find. The hickory howitzer sticks, or whatever you want to call 'em, was stacked in a neat pile and the homemade powder bags was filled and ready.

When it comes to loadin' that gun, Limber Jim takes his sweet time. First he stuffed the powder charge down the tube and then a two-foot chunk of hickory. After that he showed Mudcat how to ram them home with a pike pole. Next he turned the elevating screw ever so slow and he must've sighted six times before he was satisfied.

By this time, me and a lot of other people were gettin' edgy. There was a skiff headin' our way with two oarsmen and a man holdin' a rifle standin' in the stern. Whatever they had in mind, I was certain it wasn't good.

Limber Jim was givin' and takin' orders all at the same time. "Commence firing!" he shouted. Then he touched his cigar to the fuse and stood stiffly at attention with his left hand stuck in his shirt. I never seen anything like it.

BAARROOOOM! the ol' girl roared and the *Jessie Bill* cut a terrible dido. For a second, I thought the cannon had blowed up and we were sinkin', but it was only the recoil that made us bounce so. Limber Jim started cussin' as soon as he saw he didn't hit nothin'. But one thing was sure: he got their attention. People was poppin' out of every door and window on that boat and the the skiff almost capsized tryin' to get out of the road.

In no time at all, Argonaut swabbed the howitzer barrel, usin' a rag tied to a pole. Mudcat was right there to load and after Jim gave the elevating screw a small turn, the gun roared again. This time we had something to cheer about. The shot caught the near corner of the pilothouse, tearing away the whistle and about half the roof. Oh, it was a beautiful sight!

By now the gun crew were workin' like they were possessed. "We got the range now!" Jim yelled. He must've used more powder, because this time the racket was enough to bust your ears. When the smoke began to clear, we could see an ugly-lookin' hole amidships just above the boat deck. It wasn't long until a new batch of smoke poured out of the hole and people was leavin' that boat like the devil was after 'em. I saw several rifles but nobody stopped to use 'em; they was in too big a rush to get to the other boats.

Now the smoke from the *Hudson Bay* was a lot heavier and when a puff of flame appeared, everybody did more cheerin'. Four-Mile pounded Limber Jim over the back. "The firebox," he said. "You hit 'em smack in the firebox!" The blaze quickly spread to the upper deck, but we didn't have time to watch. Not with people shootin' at us from the *Golden Gate* and the *Hiram Price*. Wabasha Dan called for steam and we came about in a hurry, headin' east straight toward the sheer-boom. The *Golden Gate* was slowly gainin' on us and the *Price* was followin' close behind. One shot put a hole in the lazy bench and I decided right then the pilothouse was a poor place to watch the show.

I knew there wasn't time to open the sheer-boom and when we kept steamin' in that direction, I got that terrible rat-in-a-trap feeling. By now I was down in the deckhouse, which is about the safest spot on the boat. I didn't know what the plan of attack was, but I figured we had one by the way Four-Mile and Limber Jim kept makin' diagrams and sending Cleve up to talk with Wabasha Dan.

When we got near the entrance to the sheer-boom, Dan put the wheel over hard to port. We came close to climbin' the bank and that let us gain a little on our pursuers. Now we was on an upstream heading and I could tell by the vibrations that the *Jessie Bill* was runnin' faster'n she ever had before. Man, she did shake. The slough narrowed down quite a bit and Dan took advantage of the extra current when he put the wheel over as far as it would go and we came about in a tight half-circle. It was a neat maneuver, let me tell you, and it took the *Golden Gate* by surprise. Here we was on a downstream course headin' hellbent for the *Golden Gate* and her pilot had no more'n a couple of minutes to decide whether he was gonna give ground or be rammed.

By now the two boats weren't but 200 yards or so apart and as the *Golden Gate*'s nose came around, the Fort Madison Sweetheart had a broadside target.

Nobody remembered hearin' the howitzer, but that's because the sound was so puny compared to the *Golden Gate*'s boilers. There was a terrible flash of fire like lightning on a summer night and a roar that left everybody holdin' their ears. Planks and all kinds of junk came rainin' down from the sky. We could hear people screamin' on what little was left of the boat and there was others in the water, yellin' for help.

Cleve had the yawl out grabbin' people out of the water and we did the best we could for those that was hurt the worst. Everybody was so excited that we sort of forgot about the *Hiram Price*, but she was rescuin' people, too, and pretty soon somebody stepped out on the front end wavin' a white nightshirt. Pot Belly saw it first. "Lord a-mighty, they've surrendered!" he yelled.

Let me tell you, there was no more fight left in those people and when Four-Mile cupped his hands and called out that they was all under arrest, they listened. He motioned for the *Price* to come along side and as soon as we got some lines out, he ordered everybody to put their rifles in a pile. There was a bunch of them, includin' shotguns, pistols and some wicked-lookin' knives, too.

When Four-Mile takes charge, there's no nonsense. None. He sent Limber Jim and his gun crew aboard to guard the prisoners and he put Cleve up in the *Price*'s pilothouse and told him to lead the way down to Buffalo as soon as we got the sheer-boom open. We had three or four prisoners stretched out in the deckhouse and one of 'em grabbed my leg and said he wanted to talk to whoever was in charge. Right off I saw it was ol' Black Beard who had paid us a call last night. He had blood oozin' down past his ear and I could tell he was scared, so I ran and got Four-Mile.

"Who are you people anyway?" Black Beard asked. He was havin' a hard time proppin' himself up on one elbow.

"The boat brigade of the U. S. Cavalry," Four-Mile answered. "Why, there's so many thieves and cutthroats around here even the Injuns are complainin'." He made it sound convincing.

"How'd you find us?"

"We been watchin' every move you made for weeks. If you steal enough logs, sooner or later you're gonna get caught."

"Why didn't you tell us you had a cannon?"

"You didn't ask us."

"What's gonna happen now?"

"As soon as we get to Buffalo, we're gonna have a party."

"Party? What kind?"

"A necktie party, that's what."

With trembling hands, Black Beard fumbled in the lining of his cape and pulled out some bills. "Turn me loose and there's more where this come from," he said.

Four-Mile's hand closed over the money. "Much obliged. We been wantin' to buy another cannon and this is probably all we need," he said.

Chapter Twelve

River's so low I seen a catfish swimming upstream
had a bullfrog going ahead of him taking soundings.
—Ben Lucien Burman

JULY 17, 1880:

Some say it was foul play and some say he lit out of his own free will. Either way, Fatback has disappeared. Vanished. For three days we beat the bushes lookin' for him and we never found so much as a trace. The captain printed up a bunch of handbills, but not even a $100 reward turned up a shred of evidence.

Ever since, ol' Lafe has been beside himself. He blames those pirates, sayin' "dear Reginald" could have been hit by a stray bullet or fallen overboard during all the cannon fire. But I don't go along with that, not after Argonaut Smith said he was almost sure he saw Fatback after we brought the prisoners down to the Buffalo landing.

Four-Mile says there's no mystery to it: Fatback got fed up with the captain and his schemes and headed for Ohio. And if that's the way it was, he picked a good time to pull stakes. The folks of Buffalo did everything but have a parade for us. One and all, we was heroes when the town found out what had happened. People kept bringin' us food and they wanted to see the Fort Madison Sweetheart so bad they would've paid admission. The marshal, he was bug-eyed when we turned over 23 prisoners, 13 of them more or less able-bodied and 10 that needed a lot of patchin' up. They found two bodies floatin' in Pomme de Terre Chute and they got boats up there draggin' for three others.

It was all Four-Mile could do to convince the captain to give up the search for Fatback. Like Cleve says, when you got a meal ticket like that, you don't want to let go of it. It took the better part of a day to locate our raft and get it in shape. Most of our lines was still there and we was lucky to get out of the chute and headed downriver before everybody started flockin' in to claim their lost logs.

When we got to Winona, the river was fallin' fast. Things wasn't any better at LaCrosse and Lafe and Four-Mile got into a runnin' argument about how soon we ought to sell our raft. "The further we go the more money we make," the captain contended. "We got way too much invested," Four Mile said. "The further we go on a falling river, the more chance we got of breakin' up or goin' aground."

When we drug bottom at the head of Maquoketa Island, the captain began to see the light and we tied off the raft at Knapp's Mill in Dubuque. For a while, I thought the dickerin' was gonna go on the rest of the summer. First they couldn't agree on the log count and no way could they agree on the price. Then the mill people made what they said was their last offer—a down payment of $2,500 and $7,000 payable in 60 days—and we took it. I'm not too good with figures, but it looked to me that it's better to push somebody's else's raft than gamble on one of your own.

We headed back to Beef Slough and the farther we went upriver, the hotter it got. The dry weather seemed to be suckin' the life out of the river, and the *Jessie Bill*, too, for that matter. Everybody was on edge and Pot Belly and Grumble Jones got into a terrible row over some little engine noise that didn't amount to a hill of beans.

It was too hot to sleep and I was out on the front end talkin' to Cleve when we put in for wood at ol' man Dee's place below McGregor. There was a raft tied off near the point upstream and when Dee lit his lantern, I could see two men sittin' beside him on the dock. One of 'em came aboard as soon as we got the plank down and I heard him ask Lafe and Four-Mile if they wanted to take over his raft. His name was Riley and he was a buyer for the Tabor Lumber Company of Keokuk. He talked a blue streak and the captain kept backin' him up and makin' him run his words by again. The *Ben Franklin* from New Boston was bringin' the raft down from Beef Slough, and the way he told it, bad luck dogged them every foot of the way. They had one break-up and they'd run aground twice. They'd been sittin' here for nigh onto a week after the *Ben Franklin* broke down. They had a man over from Clayton, but he couldn't fix her and finally the captain gave up and headed home on one engine.

All the while he was talkin', Riley kept moppin' his face and wipin' the sweat band of his fancy hat. "Don't mind telling you there's big money riding on this," he said and that, of course, got the captain's attention. "There's not a stick of lumber to be had in Keokuk. Not one," he continued. "My company is fighting some swindler across the river at Hamilton and if we get our logs there first, we can put him out of business."

Then he paused while he caught up on his moppin'. "Trouble is this guy's bringing down a raft, too. So far, we're ahead, but at this rate we won't be for long."

Four-Mile said he didn't like the sound of it, not with all the low water. "Who's pushin' the Hamilton raft?" he asked.

Riley thought a while before he answered. "The *Crescent City*."

"Erin Murphy's boat?"

"Yeah, he's the guy they call the lightning pilot."

"He's only a thunder pilot," Four-Mile said and now we knew he was interested. "How much you payin'?"

Riley got an envelope and a stub pencil out of his pocket and started figurin'. "I'll give you the going brail price whenever you deliver the raft." Then he leaned forward and poked Four-Mile's shoulder. "And if you get there before the *Crescent City*, you'll get an extra thousand dollars."

Lafe and Four-Mile are seldom of a mind, but this time they agreed and by daylight we had that raft good and snug and was headin' downriver.

Everyday the sun beat down somethin' fierce and that made life pretty miserable when we had to start double-trippin' because of the low water. The first place was Jack Oak Bend and by the time we got down to Bellevue it was almost a regular thing. It was some better around Camanche, but we ended up double-trippin' almost the whole stretch of the Rock Island Rapids.

Even so, we was lucky because there was a lot of rafts aground. There was one in big trouble at Oquawka and I haven't figured out yet how we got past it. Burlington Island was about the worst of all and Four-Mile made us get out the gin poles and feel our way. We was there all morning and I don't suppose we made a quarter of a mile.

Everybody was wore out and when high wind stopped us cold at the mouth of the Skunk River, not even Four-Mile complained. The next day we hadn't made more'n two miles until we went aground above Dallas City. That was about the last straw. Me and Argonaut are doin' the cookin' now and when you're slavin' over a hot stove by day and fightin' logs half the night, you begin to wonder what's so fine about bein' a raftsman.

Four-Mile got the raft floatin' again, but it took two days of nothin' but sweatin' and cussin'. It was about sundown when we got everything back in shape and I was feelin' a little better, knowin' we wasn't more'n 25 miles or so from Keokuk. But then I saw Cleve and I could read bad news in his face.

"I been up in the pilothouse," he said in a low voice. "There's a raft behind us and Wabasha Dan says it looks like the *Crescent City*."

Nobody slept very good that night, let me tell you. The *Jessie Bill* was barely creepin', but as long as it was dark, there wasn't much Murphy and his bullboys could do to get around us. The *Crescent City* started ridin' our stern as soon as it was light and when the river widened above Fort Madison, we knew something was gonna have to give.

There's not too many places where you can run two rafts side by side in low water, but Murphy was crazy enough to give it a try. He swung the head of his raft to starboard and then he laid down every bit of steam he had. Wabasha Dan tried to force the *Crescent City* into the bank, but she kept comin' and I was almost afraid to watch. The front corner of her raft made a terrible grinding noise as it scraped along our starboard logs. The *Crescent City*'s wheel was churnin' up sand and mud somethin' awful and I think both rafts would've busted up if Wabasha Dan hadn't climbed the wheel and eased off with his port rudders. As it was, Murphy lost one and maybe two brails, but I guess he figured that was a small price to pay. Now the *Crescent City* had clear sailin' to Keokuk and I had a sick feelin' in my gut. Everybody on the *Jessie Bill* felt the same way except Pot Belly. "We ain't quittin' yet," he stormed. "When you got a bunch of damn fools like Murphy on the same boat, sooner or later they'll dig their own grave. You just mark my word."

Bless ol' Pot Belly's heart, he was right! We was runnin' maybe two miles behind the *Crescent City* and when we got to Rabbit Island below Fort Madison, there she was with her raft hard aground. Oh, it was beautiful! We had trouble, too, and I was scared we couldn't get past, but Four-Mile got out the gin poles again and some way we found the water we needed. Wabasha Dan doesn't go much for greeting whistles, but we all laughed when he blew one for the *Crescent City*—loud and clear—as we pulled away.

I don't mind tellin' you I had Keokuk on my mind and when Cleve got tired of my questions, he got his pencil and drew me a map. From Rabbit Island to Montrose is only about four miles. And Montrose is where the real trouble starts, Cleve kept sayin'. "It's 10 miles from Montrose to Keokuk, but most of that is rapids and Wabasha Dan told me once there's not a worse stretch of river between Cairo and St. Anthony's Falls."

"How we gonna get through a mess like that?" I asked Cleve.

"Break the raft up into small pieces and do a lot of prayin'," he said. "All we got to do is get into the rapids ahead of the *Crescent City*. In a place like that there's not enough water for them to get around us."

We was close to Upper Catfish Bend above Nauvoo when it happened. Cleve gave me his map and I was explainin' it to Argonaut when that awful racket sent a cold chill down my back. It was metal rippin' metal. The whole boat heaved and bucked like it was dyin'. I could hear steam hissin' and I was sure we was sinkin'. Pot Belly said we'd been better off if we had of. He was so upset he sat down and bawled. And that got me upset, because I hate to see a grown man cry.

"She run herself through," he said, over and over. I didn't know what he meant, but with all the excited talk, I finally got it figured out. What happened was we busted the wrist pin on the port crank and this let the piston head, the rod and the pitman go forward with such a lick that it busted the main cylinder on that side. Next to havin' the boilers blow up, runnin' through yourself is the worst thing that can happen to a steamboat. The *Jessie Bill*'s got another engine, but you can't push a raft with just one, sure.

Right off, the captain wanted to know how long it would take to fix it. "'Til Christmas, probably," Pot Belly said.

"Why can't we replace the cylinder?" the captain asked.

Now Pot Belly was mad. "Damn it, Lafe, what you don't know about boats would fill three books. When you're runnin' a boat that's only a little younger than Noah's Ark, you couldn't find the right cylinder for love nor money. You'd have to start from scratch and cast one!"

The captain went off to find his wine bottle and everybody else just stood around like they was waitin' for a funeral. Early the next mornin' we used *Jessie Bill*'s lone engine to nudge the raft a little and get her snubbed to a big cottonwood on the Illinois bank. Nobody said anything, but we all knew we had one more bitter pill to swallow. And it wasn't long in comin'. About noon the *Crescent City* come into sight. She wasn't movin' fast and her raft was a little smaller, but she was afloat. To make us feel worse, there was a light rain falling, the first in almost a month. There was the devil's brother, Erin Murphy, hangin' out of the pilothouse, wavin' and makin' hoots and catcalls with the rest of the crew as they went by. I knew right then it was the low point of my life.

It must have been Friday when Argonaut and me took the yawl down to Nauvoo for supplies. Cleve went along and we waited while he rowed across to Montrose. When he got back, he said the *Crescent City* was aground in the rapids and goin' nowhere fast.

"That's still faster'n we're goin'," Argonaut growled.

"You're right," Cleve replied. "But it's still going to take Murphy a mighty long time to make Keokuk."

Sometimes Cleve can talk up a storm and the next day he won't tell you nothin'. He kept us waitin' around Nauvoo for another two hours and all he'd say was he had to see a man on business. Then on the way home he was whistlin' some and that made me half mad. I hate people who whistle when they got nothin' to whistle about.

Cleve was gone for two days and I could tell Four-Mile knew what he was doin', but he wouldn't tell me. On Tuesday I saw this funny-lookin' boat comin' upriver and there was Cleve at the wheel, standin' by a man with a big stomach and a big bush of silver hair.

We started laughin' because the boat was so little and that didn't go down so good with Cleve when he came along side and tied up. "This is my friend, Captain Ollie Carter," he said, glarin' at us. "This is his boat, the *Quincy Adams*. She's a bow boat, a fishing boat and a lightering boat all in one, built special for the rapids. And she's here to take us to Keokuk."

There wasn't no laughin' after that, let me tell you. Cap'n Carter and Cleve's dad used to work together on the Ohio River. Over around Shawneetown. The captain retired about three years ago, but when Cleve told him the fix we was in, he said he'd help us out if he could.

People was shoutin' and askin' questions and you couldn't hear a thing. Finally, Four-Mile settled everybody down. "The canal," he shouted. "We're gonna put that dad-blamed raft through the canal."

"Whose jug you been nippin' out of, Four-Mile?" Pot Belly wanted to know. "They wouldn't let you put a raft in the canal, even if you could get it into small enough pieces."

I thought the whole thing sounded crazy. It's better'n three miles from Montrose to Galland, which is the head of the canal. The canal is seven miles long and there are three locks, the last one at Keokuk. Each lock is only 300 feet long and 80 feet wide and how you gonna get a 600-foot brail into something like that?

"You forgot the Tabors built this raft for low water," Cleve said. "Instead of having six big brails, we got eight little ones.

Each one is only 250 feet long and 45 feet wide. We'll lock 'em through one at a time."

One good thing, ol' Lafe kept out of the road and let Four-Mile run the show. The first thing we did was split the raft long-ways, makin' each piece two brails long and two wide. Cap'n Ollie will be the pilot and Wabasha Dan said he'd stay with the crippled old *Jessie*. I left a little grub for Dan. Then Argonaut and me grabbed all the pots and pans and what supplies we had and moved 'em over to the *Quincy Adams*. We tied one piece to the bank and then the *Adams* butted up against the other and we secured the lines after we got underway.

We had fairly easy goin' to Montrose, but it got bad again as soon as we hit the top end of the rapids. Every time we drug bottom, I held my breath. It was about dusk when we landed on the Iowa side a little above Galland and that's the way Four-Mile wanted it so we wouldn't have too many folks watchin' us. Then Cap'n Carter took Cleve and Limber Jim and headed back after the other piece and the rest of us started takin' our piece apart, brail by brail.

It must have been midnight when we pushed the first brail into the Galland lock. The lock-tender was sound asleep, but it wasn't long until he was jumpin' up and down and tellin' us that rafts wasn't allowed in the canal. Four-Mile demanded to see the canal regulations and after he'd read 'em twice, he wanted to know where it said anything about rafts. By now he had the lock-tender backed up against the wall and the poor man said he'd make an exception, just this one time.

I'd have to say that was about the longest night I ever spent. We had two skiffs in the lock and as soon as it was empty, we'd pull the brail out, a foot at a time. Then when the lock was filled, the *Adams* would shove in the next brail and we'd start all over again. I had blisters on top of my blisters.

It took eight lockages to get both pieces through and by day-light, I hardly had strength left to cook breakfast. Then Four-Mile said we had to have some shut-eye and everybody folded up, right on the spot. We was back at it in a couple of hours. Cap'n Carter moved the first piece down to the second lock with Argonaut and Mudcat as his crew. The rest of us started fittin' the second piece back together so it'd be ready to go.

By three o'clock the *Adams* was back and Mudcat hit the bank runnin'. "I seen two of them," he told Four-Mile, "two *Crescent City* men, maybe more. Standin' by the lock-tender's house. They're after us, sure."

That called for a council of war between Four-Mile, Cleve and Limber Jim. Cap'n Carter was there, too. I could tell by their voices they couldn't agree on what we should do. Then when they went and got Cap'n Lafe, I knew things must be pretty bad off.

I was cleanin' up the supper pots when we headed out with the second piece. Four-Mile wouldn't tell us a thing, except to say that everybody had to be out of sight before we got to the second lock. "Don't make no noise and don't do nothin' until you're told," he warned.

I was stretched out up front on the boiler deck where I could look down on the stageplank and part of the forecastle. Somebody stepped on my leg and it was Limber Jim tellin' me to be quiet. I knew Cap'n Carter was at the wheel and I could see Bush McDonald out by the plank. The light was failin' fast but when we eased along the bank, I could make out three men standin' there. The short one in the middle spoke and I knew right off it was Erin Murphy. "This canal is closed to traffic," he announced.

"This is the steamer *Quincy Adams*," Cap'n Lafe called out. "Why are you closing the canal?"

"I know your voice, Lafe Clapsaddle," Murphy shouted. "You know why we're closing the canal. And I'll tell you how we're going to do it. By putting your new boat in the lock and chopping a hole in the bottom, that's how!"

"Murphy, have you gone clean out of your mind?" Lafe asked. "I need your help in the worst way. My boat's broke down and my crew's on strike. They're trying to squeeze the last dollar out of me. All I got is my pilot here, one fireman and a kid out front who don't know beans."

At least that last part's the truth, I said to myself.

"Lafe, I never did believe a word you said," Murphy replied. "Why should I start now? We know what you're up to and no way are we going to let you use this canal to sneak past us."

"You're wrong, Erin," the captain said in a hurt voice. "Dead wrong. I'm trying to get logs to Keokuk and so are you. Let's work together and share the profit."

"Enough of your sweet talk, Clapsaddle. It's making me sick. We're going to do this my way. Get a piece of paper and start writing. I want you to authorize me to take possession of your raft and to collect all money promised to you upon delivery to the Tabor Mill. I'll give you just five minutes to think it over. Do it and you'll save this boat; refuse and you'll lose it. Remember the rest of my boys are just a little ways from here."

Lafe lit the pilothouse lamp and he called down to Bush to hang a lantern on the stageplank. "I beseech you, Murphy, don't do this to me," he said. Oh, it was good actin', I'll tell you. Ol' Leonidas Pettibone would have been proud of him.

"Quit talking and keep writing," Murphy said. Everything was dead quiet. Murphy's two sidekicks stepped into the light like they was ready to start bustin' up the boat. One carried an ax and the other was holdin' a canthook.

The pilothouse door closed and I heard Lafe slowly coming down the steps. "Do you want to read this?" the captain asked from down below. As soon as he spoke, I felt Limber Jim get to his feet.

What happened next made my head swim. Murphy let out a blood-curdling scream and I heard a rope hissin' through a pulley. Both Four-Mile and Cleve were yellin' and people were clappin' and cheerin' all over the place.

There was ol' Erin scared to death, all wrapped up in a fish net, dangling from the end of the boom on the kingpost. Four-Mile was fishin' one *Crescent City* crewman out of the canal and Cleve had the other one backed up against the lock-tender's shack.

Right off I could see Cleve's work in the whole scheme. They took one of Cap'n Carter's big nets and spread it out on the front end like a snare. Then they ran a line up to the kingpost boom and gave the end to Limber Jim up on the boiler deck. The minute Murphy stepped on the forecastle, Limber Jim went flyin' over the rail with that line and the lightning pilot got the fastest ride of his life.

Four-Mile laid it on Murphy's cronies pretty hard. "Your captain threatened to destroy this boat and we're holding him until the Lee County sheriff and his posse get here. You two men are just as guilty, but we're not going to press charges, at least not right now. But if you and your friends show up here again, then we'll have to take the law into our own hands. Understand?"

In the meantime, Murphy was hollerin' his head off for somebody to get him down. Four-Mile took his sweet time about it and then he turned him over to Grumble Jones with instructions to keep him tied. "This is kidnapping!" Murphy screamed, his face red with rage.

"No such thing," Four-Mile said smugly. "You're a dangerous man and we're just doin' our duty."

I can't explain it, but nobody was tired anymore. The locktender still hadn't appeared, but it didn't matter because by now we knew how to run the place. Everybody pitched in without Four-Mile sayin' a word and the last brail was locked through before breakfast.

It wasn't long after that until all three lock-tenders showed up, along with the sheriff and all of his deputies and more people than you could shake a stick at. I'd have to say our reception wasn't too warm. But it got better in a hurry when our man Riley arrived, along with the head man at the Tabor Mill. Right off, Riley told the whole crowd how we had slaved and suffered for the people of Keokuk.

Four-Mile had a long talk with the sheriff about Murphy and his criminal past. Murphy was spittin' mad, but everytime he tried to defend himself, Four-Mile interrupted him. "I'd recommend parole," Four-Mile said, "only because of those poor, wretched souls on his boat. They're aground over in the rapids and I look for 'em to be there the rest of the summer."

Before noon another lightering boat about the size of the *Adams* came up the canal and Riley said he thought we could do with some help. There was a bunch of Tabor mill hands on board and together we poked those brails through the lower lock in jig time.

I was out on the head end when we put the first piece back together and there was Keokuk, about the prettiest place I ever did see.

Chapter Thirteen

You can't make all your money
comin' ahead. You got to
make some of it backin' up.
—Captain Oren Russell

JULY 28, 1880:

We haven't been doin' much of anything lately and that may be one of the reasons why we tried to get into the excursion business. We was laid up in Keokuk for the better part of two weeks while Pot Belly scoured the countryside for a new cylinder to replace the one we busted above Nauvoo.

Captain Ollie towed the *Jessie Bill* down through the canal and the Tabors let us tie up at their landing. Probably you won't believe this, but Captain Lafe was as good as his word about the extra money we got from the lumber company. Everybody got an equal share of the $1,000, includin' Captain Ollie. That's why we didn't mind loafin' around Keokuk. It'd been so long since we'd had any money to spend that we needed the practice. Pot Belly had Grumble Jones and Mudcat Lewis goin' in all directions lookin' for a cylinder. He was sure we wouldn't find one and I think he was disappointed when one just the right size turned up at Warsaw, right under our noses.

As soon as they got the cylinder in place and everything workin' right, we started lookin' for what Lafe likes to call gainful employment. Ever since the first of the month, there's been precious few rafts comin' down. Part of the trouble is low water, but lumber prices have got too high and folks just ain't buyin'. A lot of raft boats are tied up and others are out there tryin' to make a nickel anyway they can. Last week we pushed coal barges from Port Byron to Camanche and day before yesterday we delivered three teams of mules to Sabula. We all wanted to head up to Beef Slough and take our chances, but I guess ol' Lafe was afraid to risk it.

But now I need to tell you about the excursion business and how the *Jessie Bill* got into it. I knew something was afoot when Professor Howe showed up at the landing, first with Petunia and the next day with Preacher Pratt. Both times they had long talks with the captain. Then they shook hands and when I saw Lafe give the professor and the preacher his back-slapping treatment, I could tell there was a big deal brewin'. Pot Belly was the first to hear about it and he spread the word with great fanfare. "It's the Annual Methodist Episcopal Praise the Lord Picnic and Barbecue and we're right in the middle of it," he announced. This brought a slew of questions and, like always, he held up his hand and said he could answer them only one at a time.

It took a while, believe me, but we finally got the straight of it. Petunia read about a big church excursion somewhere and she thought this would be a way to pump a little life into the M.E. Church's summer picnic. "I've been to 'em and they're pretty dull," Pot Belly said. Then he told how Preacher Pratt and Professor Howe put it all together. They would invite the entire town of LeClaire, give them a boat ride down to Campbell's Island and back, feed them and entertain them. And while they were doin' it, they might also win some souls and reduce the church mortgage all at the same time.

Preacher Pratt was new in town. He had a sour face and the biggest arms and shoulders I've ever seen. In or out of church, any man that big is bound to win a lot of arguments.

Pot Belly wasn't sure, but he thought both the *Stillwater* and the *Enterprise* had turned down the church proposition before they come to the *Jessie Bill*. Then he hesitated and got that funny look of his. "Maybe they're smarter'n we are," he said. Cap'n Lafe joined the circle at that point and scolded Pot Belly for sewing seeds of doubt. "Two weeks from Saturday is the day," he said. "I predict it will an historic occasion and a red-letter day for this vessel." That wasn't exactly the way he said it, but I knew for sure I'd heard it all before. Wabasha Dan Wilson promptly announced that he did not believe in picnics or prayer meetings and he would have no part in transporting Methodists or any other church-goers to such an event. Plain and simple, the rest of us thought it was a crazy scheme, but we didn't want to knock anything that might earn us a little pay.

The captain took about half the crew to a plannin' meeting in the church basement and we found out in a hurry that Petunia was running the show with the preacher as her right-hand man. There was a lot of church folks there and she had jobs for everybody, us included. Once she waved at me and a little later when she caught me lookin' at her, she gave me a wink. You can bet I steered clear of her after that. Most of the time she had three things goin' at once. She put one bunch to work paintin' signs and banners. Then she read off a long list of committees. There must have been 20 of 'em, each with about a dozen members.

First they talked about numbers and Petunia and the preacher finally settled on 150. Then they talked about money and who was going to be paid how much for doing what. Lafe said he'd need at least a dollar a head because we'd have to rent a barge to carry that many people. Preacher Pratt kept chippin' away at him and they finally agreed on 50 cents for adults and two-bits for kids. From there on, it got more complicated with each side keepin' a wary eye on the other. The way it turned out, I think the church folks beat the boat folks, hands down. The boat had to furnish the lemonade and root beer, but we got only half of the sale price. It's six miles to the head of Campbell's Island and we had to load and haul all the tables and chairs and all the rest of the stuff, makin' two trips each way. The church rented two tents for the swimmers, but we had to put 'em up and take 'em down. And worse, we had to serve the watermelon and help roast the hogs, startin' the night before.

It cost us $10 to rent a big wood flat that we could use as a passenger barge. Then we had to rig some posts and run a line around the outside so's people wouldn't fall overboard. Professor

Howe said folks might get heat stroke if the weather stayed hot and that meant we had to scrounge up a canvas fly so there'd be a little shade near the stern. All that took the better part of three days and we hadn't even made a good start. The next thing I knew we was on our way south to Muscatine to pick up the watermelon. There must have been a hundred of them and they was heavy ; I thought my arms would fall off. Since we had to come past Campbell's Island on the way home, Lafe thought it would be a good idea to land and offload the melons, so we did it all over again. Only this time we carried 'em back in the brush and covered 'em up with leaves. I didn't say nothin', but hidin' 100 watermelons seemed like a losing proposition.

Captain Lafe said I was in charge of the drinks and that killed most of Friday, the day before the picnic. Makin' lemonade is no easy job and without Ma helpin' me, I'd never got it done. Then I had to chase after Cletus Boggs and his brother, Fred, who had agreed to supply the root beer. After I tasted the stuff, I offered 'em a cent and a half a bottle, but they held out for two cents. Some of it was a little green and they said I should handle it easy-like.

After supper Friday, Lafe put Cleve in charge and sent the *Jessie Bill* down to the island with a half-crew. Wabasha Dan Wilson was on his way to Minnesota to visit kinfolk and Cleve was proud to be on his own. Limber Jim, Ercel and Argonaut weren't too keen about spending the night on the island, but somebody had to put up the tents and dig a pit for the barbecue. Two cooks from the church carried two dressed hogs aboard and they kept talkin' about all the firewood they was gonna need. Cleve heard 'em whispering and one asked the other if it was safe to be out here in the wilderness with three raftsmen after dark.

It's lucky Cletus Boggs is a Methodist because he didn't charge me for hauling the drinks to the landing. The *Jessie Bill* looked good when she rounded the point with the passenger barge on her port side a little after daylight. The barge railing was draped with bunting and there was a big red-white-and-blue WELCOME banner mounted between the smokestacks. We had eight stone crocks of lemonade and two wash boilers of root beer iced down and on board by the time the first passengers arrived a little before eight o'clock. Captain Lafe was there in his Sunday best, shakin' hands and flashin' his gold teeth. He also had Four-Mile Freeman standin' at the ticket booth just to make sure Preacher Pratt didn't get mixed up on the passenger count.

Cleve blew a long blast on the whistle as we backed out and headed downriver with more passengers than the *Jessie Bill* had ever seen before. The trip took a little more than an hour and everybody was in a good mood. There was a pleasant breeze blowing out of the southwest and the temperature was a good 10 degrees cooler than yesterday. Professor Howe gave the official welcome speech when the passengers disembarked and I blessed him for keeping it short. Then Petunia took over, herding people around and prodding them into line for a bunch of silly races and relays. Only the aged and the infirmed escaped. The rest was hoppin' around on one foot or otherwise workin' up a terrible sweat. If nothin' else, it helped the refreshment business.

Petunia had so many games goin' that she needed a helper. And who do you suppose it was? Bush McDonald, that's who. He was right there, doggin' her footsteps; in between races she was givin' him big smiles and pattin' him on the head. Once she even mussed up his hair. I couldn't believe an exhibition like that. Here's a girl that winks at me one day and carries on with a mountebank the next. And that's not all. I never saw a woman who's half as forward as she is. And half as bossy. She dearly loves to put on a loud, vulgar show in public, just like she did last March when she got smack in the middle of a riverfront brawl. All I can say it's unladylike and that's puttin' it mildly.

Campbell's Island looked better'n I had ever seen it, or at least the north end did. A section of the beach had been raked clean on the river side and two dressing rooms have been set up back in the trees, one for women and one for men. Over on the land side, the cooks were already carving up the hog roast and there was plenty of shade for the food tables. They rang the dinner bell at 11:30 and Preacher Pratt climbed up on a bench to give the invocation. Timewise, it was more like a Sunday morning sermon. While he was blessing everything in sight, I heard a funny popping noise. It got louder and faster and as soon as I looked at the root beer, I knew what it was. Bottle caps was explodin' and that sweet, foamy stuff was runnin' down my nose and drippin' off my chin. I paid for 50 bottles and by the time the last cap blew, there was only 11 left.

There was plenty of lemonade on hand, but it was hard to keep it in the shade and the ice was long gone before noon. Then the flies found it and after that I couldn't give it away. If you're curious to know what went wrong next, it was the watermelons. Limber Jim brought the bad news that pirates or other miscreants had made off with two-thirds of the melons and I'll bet it happened a few minutes after we unloaded 'em. It didn't take long to cut them up and I have to tell you, the pieces was very small.

About the time Petunia got the baseball game started, the weather got in its licks. The temperature made a big jump during the noon hour and when the wind suddenly died, a great cloud of mosquitoes settled in for a picnic of their own. Someone piled grass and leaves on the remains of the barbecue fire and now we had a choice: insects or black smoke. Even the baseball game between the Christians and the Lions failed to make it past the third inning. Someone hit a three-run homer for the Lions and the only ball disappeared in a patch of horseweeds.

The only thing left on the agenda was swimmin' and when Professor Howe sounded the dinner bell and announced the one-hour waiting period was over, there was a big rush to the dressing tents. Hardly anybody believes that old canard about gettin' cramps after a meal, but the professor is not one to take chances. He had about a dozen lifeguards on duty and I think their only job was to make sure the bathers didn't show no bare skin. One by one, the girls and ladies emerged from their tent, acting like they was cold and tip-toeing along in their bare feet to avoid the rocks and sandburs. Meanwhile, the boys and men stayed away in droves, even after the non-swimmers took off their shoes and socks and gathered on the beach for the fashion show.

Suddenly there was a woman's scream, loud enough to be heard at the far end of the island. Then there was more screams and loud voices coming from the women's dressing room. People were running in all directions and I could see Preacher Pratt shaking his fist and shouting at a gathering outside the men's tent. Little by little, we found out what all the racket was about. While donning her bathing suit, one of the ladies thought she saw an eye peering through a hole in the tent. She reported her suspicions to the preacher and when he circled through the woods, he caught not one but three peepin' toms standin' on a platform at the rear of the tent.

Preacher Pratt still had fire in his eye when he grabbed Captain Lafe by his lapels. "Lecherers! Debauchers!" he roared. "That's what you are! Only you raftsmen could have done such a dastardly deed!" At that point, poor Lafe didn't know what his raftsmen had done, and since the preacher was about three sizes bigger, he wasn't about to ask.

Four-Mile sidled up to Lafe and that gave the captain the courage he needed. He pushed out his chest as far as it would go and looked the preacher in the eye. "Don't anger me, sir. This boat departs in 30 minutes. If you have something to say, you may address me in LeClaire." That had to be one of his best and shortest speeches.

Limber Jim, Ercel and Argo knew they was in big trouble. "It seemed like good clean fun when we was pitchin' the tents," Limber Jim said. "So we built a little platform on the back side with steps at each end. Then we cut three holes in the canvas up near the top of the wall."

Argonaut's not one to talk, but this time he had something to say. "We showed it to the church cooks and it was their idea to pay so much a peek. They couldn't wait to tell people when the boat got here. Man and boy, they was lined up clear back in the woods. All we had to do was stand behind the platform, take their money and poke 'em when time was up."

"How much did you take in?" Lafe asked, shaking his head.

"$27.75, give or take a little," Ercel said. "Hell, we was so busy we never even got a peek ourselves."

Lafe couldn't stand much more and he took refuge in the pilothouse. "I'll run the boat and you keep the professor and the preacher off my back," he told Cleve. As soon as Four-Mile got all the stragglers rounded up and on board, he went up to the pilothouse and stretched out on the lazy bench. Lafe pulled away from the island a little after six o'clock and Four-Mile said he was doin' fine until he met the *Martha Washington* a mile or so above Spencer Island. They passed on one whistle and he must've let the *Jessie Bill* drift just a little too much to starboard. She bumped bottom twice and then she hit hard, pushin' up high on a sandbar. Four-Mile ran below and he and Pot Belly thought maybe they could get her off. "Your best chance is to act quick," Four-Mile said. "Wait too long and it'll just get worse."

This time they weren't quick enough. Four-Mile took the helm and for a while the old girl acted like she would come free. She moved several feet when he tried to back her off, but each time she slipped sideways and settled in again. After an hour and a half, he gave up and told Cleve and me to get the yawl. We were about a mile and a half from Rapids City and we headed upriver, taking turns on the oars. Even in low water, shovin' a yawl against the current ain't easy. By the time we could see the lights of the town, my hands was blistered and the sweat was burnin' my eyes. It took us a while to find Jack Butler's house and he wasn't what you'd call friendly when we got him out of bed and told him we needed his boat. Jack has a work boat that hauls sand and gravel, mainly. Her true name is the *Constellation,* but everybody calls her the *Big Dipper.*

Jack had one question and I knew what it was even before he could ask it. "Who's gonna pay for this and when?"

Cleve made a strong case for the *Jessie Bill* and all those stranded passengers. "I'll give you my own personal promise that you'll get your money."

"Now you sound just like Lafayette Clapsaddle," Jack said. "The answer is flat-out no."

Cleve figured all the time that Jack would help us and finally he did. "I'm not doin' this for you guys or that dead-beat boss of yours," he said. "It's only because I feel sorry for all those people stuck on your boat."

I started to ask him if he was a Methodist, then I decided that wasn't such a good question.

While we was waitin' for the *Big Dipper* to get up steam, Cleve and I loaded our yawl on board, plus several lines and all the lanterns Jack had, just in case. When the *Big Dipper* rounded to and came along side the *Jessie Bill,* I never saw so many sad-lookin' people. They was draped around the barge and sprawled all over the boat, some of 'em sleepin' and the rest of 'em crabbin' and bitchin.'" I couldn't say as I blamed 'em. You could tell they were hungry and thirsty and I knew they was wishin' they had the roast pork leavings and the lemonade, flies and all.

Four-Mile and Jack Butler talked for a little bit and after they got their lines where they wanted 'em, it was no time at all until the *Jessie Bill* was free and floatin'. Captain Lafe had gone to bed by that time and we never saw him the rest of the night. I was glad, because those passengers had a lot of unkind things to say about him and the boat and all the rest of us when we tied up at the LeClaire landing sometime after four o'clock.

By the time everybody was off the boat, it was too late to go to bed. Four-Mile and Cleve set on the forecastle for a long time. They never said much but I knew what they was thinkin'.

"What went wrong?" Chip asked.

"Better to ask what went right," Four-Mile said.

"This the worst day of your life?"

"No, but it comes mighty close."

"How does ol' Lafe get us into these messes?"

"Because we're too dumb to prevent it."

"When's our next excursion?"

"Shut your mouth!"

Chapter Fourteen

When a river is too thick to drink
and too thin to plow,
then you know it's contrary.

AUGUST 18, 1880:

I've never had too many complaints about workin' on the
Jessie Bill, but if those bedbugs come back, I'm gonna find me a
new boat. I can put up with all the hot weather and the low water,
but not them blood-suckin' insects. I don't know where we got
'em; some say Argonaut Smith brought 'em aboard, but he gets
fightin' mad when anybody mentions it. My Ma had a fit when
she heard about it. I never would've told her, but she saw the red
marks on the back of my neck. That set her off and she said I
couldn't come home until we was shut of them.

"That boat is one big boar's nest," she said. Then she started
raggin' me about sleepin' in dirty blankets and never takin' a
bath. "Swimming in the river doesn't count," she said before I
could give her an answer. I wouldn't admit it, but the crew quarters get kind of rank sometimes. Mostly, it's too many dirty socks
and oily britches.

Pot Belly's right when he says dog days are the worst time of
the year. First we had all those days when the thermometer went
over 100 degrees—I think it was six—and then it was bedbugs. I
swear you can't hardly find those critters in the daylight, but at
night they go after you somethin' fierce. They was bitin' extra

good one night and I was in a low-down black mood. I had a heart-to-heart talk with myself and I flat-out asked if I really thought this floating pigpen was better than livin' at home and eatin' my Ma's cooking. But I didn't do anything drastic and it's a good thing because I felt a heap better the next mornin'. I think that was the same day Pinhead Grant came aboard with a big armload of walnut leaves and twigs and we laughed when he told us his grandma said bedbugs can't stand the taste of black walnut. Well, the laugh was on us because she was right. We're out cuttin' walnut branches every chance we get and the stuff is piled all over the boat deck in case we run short.

Now that we've got 'em under control and I'm sleepin' better, I'm going to turn over a new leaf and lead a healthier life. When a feller gets older, he has to think about those things. There's gonna be more soap and less *Jessie Bill* coffee. That stuff's vile. I'm already gettin' my drinking water from the rain barrel instead of the river. Doc Morgan, he says river water is downright dangerous, but most people don't take him serious. Grumble Jones swears there's nothing like a cup of Mississippi river water with a little fine sand in it to tone up your system. He claims there's also a difference in rivers. Wapsipinicon water is the best for headaches and Des Moines water does wonders for an ailing stomach.

In case you're wonderin', I'm glad to say the *Jessie Bill* is again gainfully employed. Sort of by accident, we got ourselves part of a lumber raft. I got a gut feelin' it may be more'n we can handle, but at least it should be better than the Campbell's Island disaster. But first I need to tell you about Galena. Last week we talked the captain into headin' upriver and we got a hail just below Harrington Landing. When you're a mud clerk like me, a hail means nothin' but trouble. But ol' Lafe can't ever pass up a chance to earn a buck or two, so we put into shore to see what the guy wanted. He'd just sold his farm and he had two milk cows and a couple of spindly calves to take to market in Galena.

Any boat that makes regular landings has a clerk like me who goes ashore and wades through the mud to put off freight or receive whatever's bein' shipped. Livestock is the absolute worst because there's never been a cow or a pig yet that didn't make a fuss about walkin' up the stageplank. So there I am, pullin' on one end of a cow and the farmer pushin' on the other. Nobody helpin', of course, and everybody standin' around laughin'. I had to carry one of the calves on board and I won't even tell you what happened to my pants. But at least there wasn't any mud.

Truth is I didn't mind too much because Galena is a place I've always wanted to see. It's on the Fever River, which empties into the Mississippi six miles above Bellevue. Harris Slough puts you into the Fever and from there it's only five miles or less to Galena. Pa used to tell me about Galena when the lead and zinc mines was boomin'. Back in the '40s and '50s it was supposed to be the richest city in Illinois. People had big, fancy homes and most of 'em was rollin' in money.

The Fever River is pretty small, but it carries a whale of a lot of traffic and we had trouble findin' a place to tie up below town. I was scared to death the captain would make me help the farmer get his critters to the railroad yard, but Bush McDonald got the job instead. It was too late in the day for the farmer to collect his money and I think everybody was glad we had to lay over. The next mornin' I went with Cleve to buy supplies and that gave me a chance to see the town. I was impressed, let me tell you. Main Street goes on for blocks with every kind of store you'd ever want. We walked right by the DeSoto House, 200 rooms and all. I can see why they call it the fanciest hotel in the State of Illinois.

Four-Mile told me Galena is still the biggest river port above St. Louis. I believed him when I saw packets from places like Pittsburgh and Memphis. He also said I should keep an eye out for General Grant in case I meet him on the street. Over on the east side of the river is a big red-brick mansion which the town built for the general and gave him for free when he come home from the war. Pot Belly says Grant was a damn good general and a damn poor president. He knows all about politics and he's afraid Grant'll be back in '81 tryin' to sneak in for a third term.

Thanks to Four-Mile, we stayed in port for a second night. I was surprised when he told the captain a little sightseein' would be good for the crew and even more surprised when Lafe agreed. After I heard Grumble Jones and Mudcat Lewis had visited the Old Oaken Bucket Saloon, I figured that's where Four-Mile planned to do his sightseein.' During the afternoon, stories about the Old Oaken Bucket got better'n better: the dancing girls was pretty, the music was good and the drinks was cheap.

By suppertime, it was clear that most everybody was headed for the Old Oaken Bucket, except Lafe and Pot Belly, who have no fondness for saloons. Bush McDonald took a much-needed bath and Ercel Waters went to work with his barber tools. When we arrived, there was loud music inside and a crowd of people on the sidewalk. Limber Jim Gray was leadin' the way and just before he got to the door, a man with a heavy walking stick tripped him and sent him sprawling. When Jim came up swinging, this guy grabbed him, spun him around and flipped him over his shoulder. Argonaut Smith attacked from the rear and that was a big mistake. The same man turned quick as a cat and caught him in the throat with an elbow and there was poor Argo gaspin' for breath on the boardwalk. I never seen anybody so quick.

The man just stood there with his hands at his sides. "The name's Archimedes Sampson. They call me Arch for short," he said in a rasping voice. "I'd say the Old Oaken Bucket is a good place for you fellers to stay away from."

He looked to be 60 or maybe even 70. He was wearin' a droopy hat and a funny-lookin' linen duster. He had broad shoulders and very long arms. The way his belly stuck out, I don't suppose he could see his feet. His face was like old leather and his eyes was nothin' but little slits. Four-Mile came at him with fire in his eye, but Arch stopped him with a pointed finger. "Be warned, sir, that you are facing a man who has never lost a fight in 55 years. I can fight fair or foul, it don't make no difference. I can whip any 10 men in Galena and I can do the same to your boat crew, one at a time or all together."

"Who the hell do you think you are?" Four-Mile demanded.

"Some folks say I'm a crusader," he replied. "I'm crusading against booze and fools like you who drink it. Hell's bells, I could talk about it 'til I was blue in the face and nobody'd listen. But when I rough 'em up and tell 'em to stay out of sinkholes like this, well they pay attention."

"You oughta be locked up," Limber Jim said, still sittin' on the sidewalk.

"It'd take a wagonload of men to lock up ol' Arch," he replied. Then he started cacklin' like a rooster and goin' on and on about John Barleycorn and how this country was nigh to drownin' in a sea of booze. The words poured out of him so fast I couldn't catch half of 'em. Right then I knew he was crazier'n a coot.

Pretty soon he came up for air and he announced we was gonna be his guests at a place a lot healthier than the Old Oaken Bucket. I don't know why, but we let him herd us around the corner to a double storefront with a big sign that read "Rivermen's Retreat." There was 30 or 40 people in the place, sittin' at tables eatin', smokin' and playin' cards. The smoke was thick and the voices was loud. There was a couple of pool tables, a piano and a table piled with tracts and posters.

One minute Arch looked like he was gonna knock your head off and the next minute he was smilin' and pattin' you on the back. Only I never let him get that close. When things got too noisy, he'd pound on the table with his fist. "This is the home of the Sons of Temperance," he roared. "We're here to sign up you boys and then we'll send you out to spread the good word."

"What if we don't want to sign up?" Four-Mile asked.

"Don't rile me, sir," Arch said. "I might lose my temper." Then we got another oration about the Sons of Temperance and how they was gonna save us no matter what. "Hell's bells, you rivermen are the worst. Stubborn. Stupid. Can't tell you nothin'," he said. "But you're beginnin' to get the message from Arch Sampson. Them saloon-keepers are beggin' me to stay away, but I hit one or two every night and I got 'em buffaloed. I got 'em where the hair is short."

Every so often his mind would drift off and he'd get real quiet. But he'd always come bouncin' back. "Someday you boys'll brag and say you tangled with old Arch, the toughest keelboater east of St. Louis. If you're truthful, you'll say he slapped you around a little and saved you from bein' a drunkard, all at the same time."

Grumble Jones livened up the party with the comment that Arch might be a better talker than a fighter. Arch's face got red and he puffed up like a pigeon. "If you wasn't such a pipsqueak,

I'd show you something about fighting!" he said in a scornful voice. Then he went at it again, ravin' about how he cleaned up the Natchez Trace with his bare hands and how he made folks on the Ohio River forget about the likes of Mike Fink. After he quieted down, he wanted to know what boat we was on and where we was headed. Bush told him all that and a lot more. When he mentioned that Lafe liked his wine and Wabasha Dan had a taste for forty-rod whisky, Arch pricked up his ears like a bird dog.

"When the captain and the pilot are both boozers, your boat's in mortal danger!" he shouted. "This is a job for the Sons of Temperence. We've got a vigilante committee and they know what to do. We'll have 'em there at first light in the morning. Hell's bells, we'll hold a hearing and if we have to, we'll put those sots ashore."

While Cleve tried to push the rest of us out the door, Four-Mile and Arch just stood there nose-to-nose. I guess it was more like belly-button-to-belly-button.

"We don't want no vigilantes," Four-Mile said.

"You'll get 'em anyway," Arch replied. Then they slowly backed away, still staring at each other.

When we got back to the boat, Cleve routed out the captain and told him about where we'd been. Ol' Lafe wasn't much interested until Cleve got to the part about the vigilante committee. Then he got upset and started wringin' his hands. "How can we stop them?" he asked.

"Leave tonight, right now," Cleve said.

The captain balked, sayin' it was too dark and the river was too narrow to run tonight. But Cleve wore him down. "Just trust me, captain. I can do it," he said. So we got up steam and slipped our mooring lines a little after one o'clock. I couldn't believe how black it was. I felt like sayin' that not even Wabasha Dan Wilson could find his way, but I kept still. Cleve had us on a slow bell and as we dropped around the first bend, there was a funny kind of glow in the sky. It kept gettin' a little brighter and finally I whispered to Cleve, "What is that?"

"Fireflies, boy," he laughed. "Plain old-fashioned fireflies. Didn't you notice 'em as we were walking back to the boat? I never saw them so thick."

If that didn't beat all. There they were, clouds of 'em lightin' up the trees on both sides of the river and leavin' *Jessie Bill* a nice black ribbon in between to run on. I've heard dozens of people talk about pilotin' a boat by moonlight, but I'll bet this is the first time anybody ever did it by lightning bugs!

Chapter Fifteen

*A riverboat pilot is the only
unfettered and entirely independent
human being on earth.*
              —Mark Twain

SEPTEMBER 12, 1880:

Workin' on the river, you meet a lot of strange people, but I'll
be surprised if I ever run into the likes of Archimedes Sampson.
Cleve gets tickled every time we talk about him. He calls him
Captain Hell's Bells, King of the Keelboaters. I halfway expected
that ol' buzzard to come after us when we left Galena. I know
I've got an extra supply of imagination, but I could see him
standin' out on the roof of a big sidewheel steamer, wavin' his
broadsword and yellin' for us to surrender.

By the time we cleared the Fever River and headed up the
Mississippi, it was rainin' a little and there wasn't no fireflies to
help us. We couldn't find a good place to tie up, so we sort of felt
our way along the Iowa shore, knowin' that's where the channel
was supposed to be. Once we spotted the foot of Nine-Mile
Island, we made the crossin' and found good water on the Illinois
side. Cleve said it was about 4:30 when he saw somethin' big
comin' at him. He put the wheel over hard and we got past without hittin' it. The sky was gettin' light in the east and there was
one of the biggest lumber rafts I've ever seen, busted up pretty

bad and blockin' the channel between Shinkles Island Bar and the head of Nine-Mile Island.

The *Betsy Ross* had just made the bend when her raft rode up on the head of Shinkles Bar and split in two. She was 11 strings wide and six of 'em stayed in the channel while the other five went to the right into Mold Slough. A real mess, I'll tell you. There was no place to go, so Cleve eased us in on the *Betsy*'s port side. Two men was on the forecastle, goin' at it hot and heavy. One was tall with hair like a brush hog and the other was a little guy with hardly any hair at all. The way they talked, the big guy must have owned the lumber raft and the little guy was the boat captain or pilot, or maybe both.

"Is your boat for hire?" the big one called.

"Yes, if the price is right," Lafe replied.

"You keep still and let me do the talkin'," Four-Mile whispered to the captain. Before Lafe could respond, Mr. Brush Hog came aboard and introduced himself as Charlie Lynch from St. Louis. He was wearin' plain clothes and boots with a hole in one toe, but he had a gold chain around his neck and shiny rings on both hands. He was also packin' a big revolver on his left hip. "They call me Lucky," he said, "but my luck's been all bad since I got mixed up with the *Betsy Ross*. You people know anything about lumber rafts?"

"Enough to do the job," Four-Mile said.

"It better be more than Billy Hyde there," the Brush Hog said. "We've had grief all the way from West Newton. His boat ain't big enough. I don't want any more trouble. I'm going to break this thing into two rafts and if you can keep it together and get it down to Grafton in 10 days or less, I'll pay you three dollars per thousand board feet."

Lafe let out a couple of sounds before Four-Mile jabbed him in the ribs. "Three and a half and we'll do it," Four-Mile countered.

"You're gougin' me. Even three is more'n the job's worth."

"I'm not sayin' what the job's worth; I'm just tellin' you what we'll do it for."

Finally the Brush Hog agreed, sayin' he didn't have much choice. "But if you have a break-up, the deal's off. You tie up the raft and you get no pay. Understand?"

I'd better stop right here because I don't suppose you know much about lumber rafts. Don't feel bad; I'd never seen one up close before. All of us on the *Jessie Bill* are strictly log people, except Four-Mile. A couple of years after the war he worked on the *Fort Dearborn* and she was one of the first boats to move lumber rafts.

With lumber rafts, you saw up the logs first instead of last. I guess they call it dimension stuff—boards, planks, beams and everything you can think of, all cut to different lengths and sizes. When you got all the sawin' done, you build yourself a crib. Each crib is 32 feet long and 16 feet wide. You start out with a framework and you stack the lumber on top, first crosswise and then lengthwise. You keep doin' that until you get it as thick as you want, more if there's plenty of water and less if the stage is low. You use wooden pins and wedges to hold it together. Then you bunch up the cribs any way you want to and fasten 'em with lines, just like on the log rafts. When you line up the cribs one behind another, you've got yourself a string. The *Betsy Ross* started out with a raft that was 11 strings wide and 12 cribs long. Just to show you how good my arithmetic is, that's 176 feet wide and 384 feet long. Now you got the picture.

It took a day and a half to round up the stray cribs and patch up the few that was busted. The *Jessie Bill* worked with the downstream cribs and it was another half day before we got 'em lined up and tied in, 6 strings wide and 11 cribs long. Ol' Brush Hog pushed us hard to get movin' but Four-Mile wouldn't budge 'til he had everything just the way he wanted it. It had rained some every day and we was all wet and worn out. On top of that, we was all snappin' at each other. Ol' Pot Belly was steamed up like only he can get, and I knew I'd have to listen. "Just how dumb can this boat get, I'm askin' you?" he said. "Here we are with a lumber raft that we don't know nothing about and we're taking it way down river to a place we've never been before. That's lunacy, pure lunacy."

At first Cap'n Lafe was pleased about the whole thing, but he changed his tune in a hurry when he remembered Wabasha Dan Wilson was not on board and we didn't know when he was comin' back. He was wringin' his hands when he told the first mate we should reconsider, but Four-Mile just laughed at him. We left at first light the next morning, glad to get away from the Brush Hog and the *Betsy Ross*. I could tell Cleve was a little jumpy, pilotin' his first lumber raft. For the first hour or so, Four-Mile stood right behind him in the pilothouse, watchin' all the lines and gettin' the feel of the raft. Then they both relaxed some and Cleve gave the engine room a full-ahead bell.

We got into shallow water when we raised Savanna about dinner time and that told us there could be trouble when we tried to make the bend below Sabula. Cleve knew what he had to do and he eased the raft into the bank where the trees was big enough to tie off. Then he called for Ercel Waters and me and we all set out in the yawl to look for decent water. That's a slow process, let me tell you; especially when the sun's beatin' down and there's no breeze blowin'. Cleve had the oars and when he gave me a nod, I took soundings with the spike pole. When there was enough water to get by, Ercel stuck markers in the sand and we inched our way along until the danger of runnin' aground was past. The river was still on the low side when we got down to Elk River Slough and we tied up there for the night, just to be on the safe side.

It rained hard after midnight, giving us the little extra water we needed. Cleve said we should reach the upper rapids by late afternoon and that worried him some because he knew ol' Lafe wouldn't want to hire a rapids pilot. In fact, Cleve hardly spoke a word all day, but when we made LeClaire, he broke out in a big smile. There was Wabasha Dan Wilson, neat as a pin, waitin' for us at the Green Tree Hotel. He stood there like a statue with a satchel in one hand and a cheroot clinched in his teeth. Cleve gave him a long greeting whistle and very likely Cap'n Clapsaddle heaved a big sigh and opened a new bottle of wine.

With the river risin' like it was, we cleared the upper rapids in good shape. "Even the captain could have brought us down this time," Ercel Waters laughed. The same thing was true when we reached Montrose at the head of the lower rapids. About a mile below the town we could see a boat sittin' in about six feet of water close to the Iowa bank. One chimney was down and she had a bad starboard list. Two boats were tied up nearby and there was a crowd of people on shore. "It looks like the *Henrietta*," Wabasha Dan announced. "I reckon she hit Mechanic's Rock. Too bad."

Every riverman above St. Louis knows about Mechanic's Rock. It got its name when the steamer *Mechanic* hit it and sunk back in 1830. Nobody knows how many others did the same thing. One of 'em was the *Illinois,* a fancy packet boat which broke up there in 1842. It don't look like much because it only sticks up about two feet in normal water. But they say it's a giant boulder that weighs maybe 10 tons. According to Dan, some people wanted to dynamite the rock and others wanted to keep it because it acts as a gauge and tells you when you can run the rapids and when you should use the canal.

Mostly Dan won't give you the time of day, but he can talk your leg off if it has something to do with river navigation. He said that rock has put the fear of the Lord into a lot of pilots, him included. "Remember, there's a two-foot drop for every mile of rapids. It's swift and shallow and there's that damnable rock sittin' in the narrow entrance channel right where you don't want it." After 10 minutes of silence, Dan closed the subject with one last comment. "That rock's been there for ten thousand years, but cover it with water and some idiot like the *Henrietta* will hit it five minutes later."

We rolled past Nashville and Sandusky like the rapids wasn't even there. The canal didn't have a single customer and everybody was out in the river enjoyin' all the good water. We stopped for some tools and other stuff at Keokuk and Four-Mile had everybody out on the raft tightenin' a few lines and checkin' all the rest. He was in a good mood for a change, talkin' to the raft and tellin' her how sweet and how well-behaved she was. Lookin' back, I think those was the last pleasant words I heard for the better part of a week. I've been on the *Jessie Bill* long enough to know that when things have been goin' good for three or four days, then you'd better look out, because trouble is comin'. And it'll come where you least expect it. But I'm never ready and I sure wasn't this time.

The weather was just right and we was makin' good time on a rising river. We had just met the *Sucker State*, an upbound packet, near Kusie Island and we was near the foot of Fox Island Bar when all hell busted loose. There was a terrible thump, followed by a kind of grinding noise and then the whole boat shook like a wet dog. I'd never been snagged before, but you know what it is when it happens. It turned out to be a big one, a whole tree with a couple of limbs stickin' out at right angles. The blame thing was moseyin' along under the surface, just lookin' for a victim. Usually a raft will knock those big snags out of the way, but this one must have rolled along the bottom and popped up just in time to punch one of those limbs through the hull.

Cleve was in the pilothouse at the time and he told me Wabasha Dan Wilson never said a word. Not even a cuss word. He spun the wheel and headed for the slack water on the Missouri side, shoving the raft into the willows as best he could. It takes a while to get a raft stopped, you understand. *Jessie*'s stern got lower and lower and you could tell she was takin' a lot of water. Four-Mile was yellin' orders in that voice of his and it wasn't long until Limber Jim and Argonaut got the head of the raft snubbed to a big cottonwood. The boat slowly settled into the mud with the water runnin' a couple of inches over the main deck. It gave me a sick feelin', but I guess it could have been worse; the hole was aft on the port side and not up against the bank where we couldn't get to it.

There was just enough daylight left to secure the raft and get her tied down from stem to stern. It took about all the line we had and Four-Mile was worried the wind would come up during the night. I guess most of us was a little surprised that anything bad could happen to us when Dan was at the helm. But Four-Mile said snaggings was one of the hazards that went with the job. "You might be the world's best pilot, but sooner or later you'll have an accident," he said. "There are too many things you can't control." Then he told us about some pilot on the old *Harvest Moon* who sort of kept score. If he thought he'd gone too long without a mishap, then he'd hit somethin' on purpose and make like it was an accident. "That way, he kept the odds in his favor," Four-Mile added.

Captain Lafe played the whole thing to the hilt. The snaggin' upset him but it also told him that bad things can happen to Dan just like the rest of us and he couldn't resist rubbin' it in a little. We was havin' a late supper when Dan came in and sat down at the end of the table. "I figured you've been slippin' for a long time, Mr. Wilson, and this proves it," ol' Lafe said. "Being on vacation for so long, I suppose you got a little rusty." Pot Belly choked on his coffee and it took him a minute to get his breath. Wabasha Dan never spoke a word, but his eyes got big and we knew he was about to explode. Lafe saw it, too, and he hurried off to his cabin just in the nick of time.

It started to rain that night and it kept at it, off and on, most of the next day. Patchin' up the boat was Four-Mile's job and he didn't waste any time. As soon as it was daylight, he asked Cleve to take the yawl and see if he could locate a pump at Alexandria, about three miles upriver. He also wanted some new check line and a couple bags of oakum. Then he grabbed Bush and told him to go along and bail out the rainwater. The only thing we had plenty of was lumber and Four-Mile didn't skimp a bit. First he had us build a crude platform using planks and square timbers for legs. Then we lowered it into the water and drove the legs into the mud so we could reach the busted hull and have a place to work. Grumble Jones took over from there and built what he called a bulkhead over the jagged hole near the stern. Most of it had to be done by feel and it took a lot of cuttin' and sawin' and cussin' as well.

Cleve and Bush returned in the middle of the afternoon and that's when the real work began. Four-Mile got the pump hooked up and we took turns runnin' it—30 minutes at a crack. That doesn't sound like much, but a half-hour on that monster about did me in. And the way it was rainin', it looked to me like more water was runnin' in than we was pumpin' out. Those that weren't pumpin' got to try their hand with a cross-cut saw. Leave it to Four-Mile to keep everybody busy. He said since we'd be needin' firewood soon, he hoped the owner of the raft wouldn't mind us usin' a few of his beams and planks. It was near dark before we could tell we was makin' any headway with the pump, so we kept at it all night. And the way the river was risin', it was a good thing we did. By morning the old girl was on an even keel and her main deck was above water by a couple of feet or more.

Along toward noon we could see a raft comin' down and it turned out to be the *Betsy Ross*. When she got close, three men climbed into a yawl and come along side. Standin' up in the bow was Mr. Brush Hog, wearin' a poncho and a wide-brimmed hat. "I had a gut feeling you people couldn't handle a lumber raft," he said as he climbed up on the forecastle. "Remember what I told you. The deal is off. I'm reclaiming this half of the raft and you can leave it right where it sits. I want you out of here as soon as you get this old wreck running again."

"Just a damn minute, mister," Four-Mile bellowed from the boiler deck. He came down the ladder three steps at a time, a sure sign he was close to the boiling point. "You told us there'd be no deal if we had a break-up. Well, there ain't no break-up. We hit a snag and as soon as we get the boat fixed, we'll be on our way. And you better have the money ready when we make delivery."

"I said the deal is off. If you move this raft, I'll have you jailed."

"Will you have me jailed if I throw you off this boat?" Now Four-Mile was beginnin' to enjoy himself.

"Just try it and find out."

Four-Mile moved slowly forward and when his nose was only a couple of feet from the Brush Hog's, his face lit up and his smile got bigger and bigger. Quick as a wink, his hand caught the man's hat brim and pulled it over his eyes. At the same time he gave him a shoulder to the mid-section and the Brush Hog hit the water with a loud splash.

"Back to work!" Four-Mile shouted. Then he doffed his cap and gave our visitor a low bow while his cohorts pulled him into the *Betsy Ross*' yawl.

By suppertime, most of the water had been pumped out of the hull. After we cleaned up the sand and mud on the boat deck, Grumble crawled into the hold and started repairin' the hole from the inside. I can tell you that was a miserable job because they had me down there, too, holdin' the lantern. The air was bad and it was so hot we could hardly breathe. He finished it up the next morning, fillin' all the seams and cracks with oakum. As far as I could tell, ol' *Jessie* was almost as good as new.

A long time ago I heard my Pa say that on the river it's either feast or famine. Now I know what he meant. Just a few days ago we was out in the yawl scratchin' around in the sand tryin' to find enough water to float us and now we got more water'n we can handle. It rained off and on during the night and at breakfast time it was comin' down hard enough to drown a duck. By the time we got steam up, the current was putting strain on our mooring lines. Four-Mile worked the raft over good and when Limber Jim let the head lines go, we was off to a running start. We made Canton a little after noon and by three o'clock we was past LaGrange and comin' up on Hogback Island. That's where the cloudburst caught us and there was times when you could hardly see the bank. It let up near Cottonwood Island, thank the Lord, and that helped us make the bend and get through the Quincy bridge.

Below Quincy, the river was spreading into the lowlands and a lot of islands had nothin' showin' expect the tops of the willows. Four-Mile figured the current was runnin' a good 5 miles an hour. With that and all the rain, it was pretty plain that we'd better tie up if we planned on survivin' the night. But gettin' it done ain't so easy, not when you're chasin' a big pile of lumber down a fast-runnin' river. Wabasha Dan found what he was lookin' for at McDonald Chute, maybe four miles above Hannibal. The chute hung along the Illinois bank for a half mile or so and then curled in behind Amstrong Island where there was a little protection from the current and the wind. Mooring was the hard part and Four-Mile and his deckhands had to use the yawl to reach trees that was stout enough to hold us.

The next day was a killer, let me tell you, and I won't forget it for a long time. Right from the start, it was spooky. It was still rainin', of course, with a little fog mixed in, and all you could see was water. And I mean everywhere. Armstrong Island was gone, or at least that's the way it looked, with only some treetops to show you where it had been. What we thought was a quiet chute was now a ragin' torrent carryin' uprooted trees and logs of every size. Breakfast turned into a council of war with Wabasha Dan, Four-Mile and Cleve doin' the talkin'. Captain Lafe was present, but he never once opened his mouth except for food. Four-Mile said the river was risin' about a foot an hour and they all agreed that the *Jessie Bill* was in big trouble whether she kept goin' or tried to ride it out.

There was a long silence. All of a sudden, I was scared and I think everybody else was, too. Wabasha Dan broke the spell when he gulped the last of his coffee and headed for the door. "Let's get started," he said. And nobody disagreed.

Four-Mile said the current was runnin' better'n 6 miles an hour and it jerked the raft around some when we came out of McDonald Chute. But Dan got her straightened out in time to make the bend and line up for the Hannibal bridge. It was a fast ride and everybody cheered when we made a dead-center run under the span.

I could tell Cleve was as nervous as a cat, just from the way he talked. "People say Dan's crazy, but I never believed it until now. He's the only pilot in the world who would tackle this kind of a river," he said. "This is not a boat pushing a raft; it's a hell-bent raft running away with a boat."

Then he told me I'd better come up to the pilothouse if I wanted to get in on the action. That was all the invitation I needed and I grabbed my bucket and cleanin' rags just in case somebody tried to boot me out.

It was a weird lookin' river, let me tell you. More like an ocean. There was places where it was at least two miles wide. Maybe more. I just wish somebody'd tell me how Wabasha Dan knew where we was. He used to run this stretch of river regular, but I'll bet it never looked like this. Dan never gets excited and he doesn't talk much, but today it seemed to me he was chewin' on that cheroot a little harder than usual. Half the town of Louisiana appeared to be under water when we cleared the railroad bridge there a few minutes before noon. It's 18 miles from Hannibal to Louisiana and Cleve said we made it in less than two hours. Most of the time ol' *Jessie* couldn't do that good even when she was a lightboat.

We were almost to Clarksville when Cleve nudged me and pointed toward the Missouri shore. There was the *Betsy Ross* and three or four cribs of lumber hung up in a grove of trees. A big piece of her raft was piled up against a bluff, close enough that we could see the fast water tearing it to pieces. There was a short string floating free on the Illinois side and a thick layer of loose lumber swirling around the head of our raft. I got weak in the knees just watchin'.

Wabasha Dan was shakin' his head. And he was also talkin' for a change. "They tried to hold her back and you can't do that when you've got a raft in fast water," he said. "All you can do is drive her and get all the speed you can. When you slow down or try to flank, then you're dead. The fast water's pushing you from all sides and even if you know where the river is, you can't hold the raft there very long." That was my piloting lesson for the day and I'm sure I won't forget it.

Dan was callin' for steam a good bit of the time and knowin' this boat, I'm surprised she held up. Pot Belly worked his butt off in the engine room and he told me later that the boiler breechings were practically red hot clear to the top of the jackets. Dan also got a workout fightin' the big wheel. Almost every time we made a bend, he had a battle on his hands. The current would grab the raft and try to swing her, but he always found a way to get her head back where it belonged. We had several close calls, believe me, and the worst one was just above the village of Kampville. The current was pushin' us toward the Missouri bank when the the left front corner of the raft came rarin' out of the water. The whole raft started swingin' sideways and I thought we was gonna break up for sure. But then the corner dropped back just at the last second and Dan coaxed her around and got her goin' straight.

Captain Lafe hardly ever comes to the pilothouse when Dan is on watch, but he showed up in the middle of the afternoon and stayed only long enough to pose one question. "If we ever get this raft to Grafton, Mr. Wilson, how in the name of heaven do you plan on stopping it?" he asked and he was out the door before Dan could reply. It seemed like a good question to me and it struck me funny that Lafe could be the only one who'd thought of it. Grafton is located at the mouth of the Illinois River and that meant we'd have two flooding rivers to deal with. Dan pulled out his watch and announced we ought to make Grafton by six o'clock, but he didn't say anything about a landing.

About 5:30, a yawl pulled along side and dropped off a passenger. He talked a while with Lafe and then he climbed up to the pilothouse and introduced himself as Captain Crenshaw. "I operate a work boat for the Riley Lumber Company of St.

Louis," he said, "and I'm here to receive your raft." He was a pleasant man with a round face and a round belly. He was also talkative and he had a bushel of questions about what he called our "noble achievement." Then he grabbed Dan's hand and started pumping it. "You, sir, have made rafting history today." I could tell Dan wanted to throw the guy out of the pilothouse, but instead he just bit his tongue.

Cleve was a little more courteous and he told Crenshaw about the trouble we'd had with the Brush Hog after he hired us to take over half of his lumber raft. "You mean Lucky Charley Lynch," he said. "He's a buyer for our company and he's also a blowhard. Forget about him. He didn't do so good with his half of the raft and right now he's unemployed."

As soon as Grafton came in sight, we knew it was going to be a very wet landing. Our new pilot took us north across the top of Mason Island and told Dan to head inland when we got to the far bank of the Illinois River, a few hundred yards above the flooded village. "Don't worry," Crenshaw said. "We're over the baseball field right here and behind it is a pasture. Point for that barn and get your bow on this side. It's sloping ground and when the raft hits bottom, give her a good push and then you can drop it right there."

That sounded easy, but we was comin' ahead slow and when Dan tried to hold the raft against the current, all of a sudden he didn't have enough power. All we could do was watch as the bow swung in an arc and whacked off the second floor of the barn right at the waterline.

Dan was boilin' mad and Cleve and me knew better than to try and console him. Just the same, we agreed that there'd never be a pair like the *Jessie Bill* and Wabasha Dan Wilson. Who else could team up to take a lumber raft 198 feet long and 80 feet wide down 95 miles of flooded river and hit nothing but a barn?

Chapter Sixteen

RAFTSMAN JIM

So her pop sez 'Nay,'
And he lopes away,
And bobs right back the very next day,
And he shuts one eye,
And looks very sly;
She gives to her pop the sweet bye-bye.

CHORUS

There ain't no cub as neat as him—
Dandy, handy Raftsman Jim.

OCTOBER 25, 1880:

A lot of folks said it was one of the best celebrations LeClaire
ever had. Almost as good as when Lee surrendered at
Appomattox. I don't think I ever had more fun in my whole life,
or more surprises. Let me tell you, I got a surprise every time I
turned around. And it wasn't just the town of LeClaire; it seemed
like the whole countryside turned out. There was two boatloads
of people from Davenport, includin' the Scott County Boys
Marching Band in their new red hats and black plumes.

The landing was almost solid with boats; the wagons and bug-
gies was about as thick as fish flies on the Fourth of July. There
was a long string of tables, all of them loaded down with vittles.
They also had big crocks of ice tea and lemonade. Somebody

said there was beer, too, but our crew didn't mention it and if there'd been any, they'da found it.

It's hard to believe that people did all this just for the crew of the *Jessie Bill*. You talk about miracles, why as long as I can remember everybody made fun of ol' *Jessie* and there was a lot of folks in this town who wouldn't even admit there was such a boat. But all that changed after we broke up that pirate ring in Pomme de Terre Slough. At first there wasn't much said about it and then all of a sudden the newspapers was full of it. And I mean big papers, like the *Chicago Tribune* and the *St. Louis Globe*. Some of the stories was doctored up a little, but that just made us look all the better.

Back in June we could hardly live with ourselves. Folks was shakin' our hands or pattin' us on the back and we loved every minute of it, all but Wabasha Dan Wilson, that is. Then in July we got involved in that awful Campbell's Island excursion trip and we was sure the whole town was mad at us, or at least everybody at the M.E. Church was. Maybe a lot of folks didn't know about that mess or else they decided to forgive us. Anyway, I could hardly believe it when I heard the mayor was talkin' about a celebration in our honor. He got the idea after the directors of the Mississippi River Logging Company at Beef Slough voted to give us the reward money they put up for the arrest of the log thieves. Next thing we knew, the Governor of Wisconsin issued a special proclamation citing the *Jessie Bill*'s crew for courage and bravery and a bunch of other stuff. The whole thing sorta snowballed and it wasn't long until Captain Lafe got a hand-delivered invitation spellin' out all the honors we was due to receive on Sunday, October 10, 1880 A. D. at two o'clock in the LeClaire City Park.

Business was bad and we had some time on our hands in July, but things got better in August and we brought down two rafts from Beef Slough, both for the Tabor Mill. The first one was mostly trouble because of low water at Hanging Rock above Prairie du Chien. There was four or five rafts stacked up and we sat there for most of a week before we got a rise. Four-Mile was right when he said there's bound to be trouble when you get more'n one raft crew in the same town. Two crews got into a ruckus one night in Prairie du Chien and when Limber Jim heard about it, he couldn't wait to go watch the fun. Ercel Waters went with him the next night and when they got back to the boat, Limber Jim said they was lucky to get out of town alive. "Pure carnage," he called it.

There was six the next night and this time they went to Marquette, across from Prairie du Chien on the Iowa side. Somebody told 'em Marquette was a peaceful place where the marshal didn't allow no fightin'. Four-Mile said the marshal must have been gone because by the time they got there, 15 or 20 raftsmen were doin' battle in the middle of the street. Before the night was over, they wrecked one saloon and burned down the livery stable. Most of our boys was bunged up pretty bad, includin' Mudcat Lewis who lost two teeth. "You shoulda been there," Mudcat told me and Cleve. "You'da loved it."

We had better water for the second raft, but we made the mistake of goin' all the way to Stillwater and there wasn't nothin' stirrin' on the St. Croix. After about 10 days or so, we gave up and we had to run lightboat clear to West Newton before we got a raft. I've already told you about September and the flood and our wild and wooly trip down to Grafton with a lumber raft. It was fast and it was excitin', but I'd be lyin' if I said I was ready to do it again.

We spent three days gettin' ready for the celebration, doin' unheard of things like cleanin' up the boat and paintin' a little here and there. Most of us had new haircuts and clean clothes, but nobody was prepared for all the fuss and feathers when we tied up about ten o'clock at the LeClaire landing.

There was Professor Howe, decked out in a new suit, waitin' to greet us. This time he wasn't ashamed to have people know he was one of the *Jessie Bill*'s owners. Petunia was right beside him with a big bouquet of flowers which she presented to Captain Lafe. She gave me a big smile and asked a lot of questions, of course. I was scared she'd tag after me all day, but she didn't and Cleve said that's because my new status as a hero made her shy for a change.

You can bet my Ma was there. I was a little embarrassed when she hugged and kissed me, but it still felt good. All my little brothers and sisters seemed one or two sizes bigger'n when I saw 'em last. There was a bunch of uncles, aunts, and cousins, too. And it made me proud that my big brother Matthew had come all the way from Dubuque just to shake my hand.

Marshal Raintree was there, too, and I did my best to steer clear of him. But as soon as we finished stuffin' ourselves with food, he rounded up the *Jessie Bill* crew and marched us to our places in the bandstand. I never looked at him once and if he remembered takin' a shot at me when I busted out of his jail, he never let on.

Professor Howe led off the program by comparin' the *Jessie Bill* to the *Monitor* in its battle with the *Merimac* in 1862. Personally, I thought he laid it on a little thick. Then he introduced each member of the crew and I could feel my face burn when I stood up and he called me his prize pupil.

The mayor was next and since he was the master of ceremonies, it was his duty to introduce all the dignitaries present. I'm still not sure what a dignitary is, but let me tell you there was a bunch of 'em. I dozed off a time or two and that's why I don't remember all the speakers. But I was wide awake when the president of the Mississippi River Logging Company started talkin' about the *Jessie Bill* and the valiant members of her crew. I ate up every word of it! When he was finished, he gave us a fancy plaque with an inscription praisin' our "fearless efforts to maintain law and order on America's inland waters." Next came the grand prize: a reward check for $750.00! Everybody stood up and cheered and the *Jessie Bill* folks cheered the loudest of all!

You can probably guess who the mayor called on next: "Captain Lafayette Clapsaddle, master of the steamer *Jessie Bill* who will respond on behalf of members of the crew. . ." He was in his glory, and that's about the kindest thing I can say. He was dressed fit to kill and he kept on wavin' to the crowd after they quit clappin'. Then he took out his prepared speech and hooked his spectacles over his ears and I settled down for another nap.

There's no tellin' how long the captain would've talked, but his speech was interrupted by a melodious steam whistle that came rollin' up the valley. The notes sounded again, each one a thing of beauty. Every person in the crowd knew right off that it was a large boat and one strange to these waters. Folks began to stir when the steamboat came into view downstream; I reckon they couldn't help themselves. At first, only a few left their seats but before long there was a rush and they all headed for the landing. Ol' Lafe ain't one to give up easy, but when he turned around and seen he was the only one left on the platform, he stuffed the speech in his pocket and stomped off in disgust.

There for all to behold was the *New Union Victory*, a big side-wheeler that towered above the *Jessie Bill*. I knew there had to be a special word for her and Cleve said majestic would do nicely. She was painted a dazzlin' white with red trim and a big red letter "G", maybe 5 feet high, mounted between the stacks. Suddenly her calliope struck up "Oh, Them Golden Slippers" and she made a flawless landing at the upper end of the levee. People was pushin' and shovin' to get in close and three or four had to be fished out of the river. Pretty soon one of the officers came out on the forecastle with a megaphone and called to the crowd. He said he was sorry, but there was too big a crowd and it would be unsafe to let everybody aboard. After the calliope played another tune, the man with the megaphone came back. "We understand you are honoring the steamer *Jessie Bill*," he called. "The captain would like to invite those of her crew to come aboard for a brief tour."

You can bet we was all waitin' when they lowered one stage-plank and it didn't take us long to climb the grand stairway to the main salon on the boiler deck. Not even in a picture book have I ever seen anything so plush. The carpet seemed like it was ankle deep. The room was full of big fancy chairs and sofas and there was huge paintings hangin' from the bulkheads.

Waitin' at the head of the stairs was another officer, wearin' a dark blue uniform with "Purser" lettered on his cap. One look and I had him pegged. Four-Mile spotted him, too, and he hollered "Hoppin' Bob!" in a voice that everybody must've heard ashore. It was the same Hoppin' Bob that let me into Vicksburg Annie's place in Wabasha and my first thought was to go hide somewhere. But Hoppin' Bob was already talkin' up a storm with Four-Mile.

"You and Miss Annie are back on the river. I can't believe it," Four-Mile said, beatin' his friend over the back. "The *New Union Victory.* Why sure. I should've known as soon as I seen your name board."

"You got the picture, pardner," Bob said. "And what a boat it is."

"Where is she, Bob?" Four-Mile asked. "It's been a long time. I'm dyin' to see her."

Hoppin' Bob only pointed and Four-Mile let out a whoop when he saw her comin' across the salon. It was the same Vicksburg Annie, long gown, jewelry, mustache and all.

"Sweetheart, baby!" Four-Mile roared and he went for her with both arms extended. But Miss Annie did a little sidestep and offered him nothin' but her hand.

All of a sudden Four-Mile was subdued. "Annie, you haven't forgotten your old friends, have you?" he asked.

"Of course not, Four-Mile. How could I ever forget you? But things are different now.

Four-Mile tried a new tack. "Annie, how long you been back on the river? Where did you find a boat like this?"

Miss Annie was very proper and I could see there wasn't gonna be any huggin' and kissin' on this visit. "This used to be the *Admiral Curtis*," she replied. "For years it ran in the Pittsburgh trade. After we bought it, we had it completely rebuilt at the Howard yards in Jeffersonville. I suppose you could say we're tramping. We've only been out for two weeks."

"You must be back in the big money, Annie," Four-Mile said.

"Yes, you could say that, thanks to my husband."

Four-Mile looked like he was havin' a stroke. "Husband?" he croaked.

"You have to understand that things have changed," Annie said. "We were married right here in the salon the day we started our cruise."

Then she waved and this skin-and-bones figure headed our way, shufflin' across the carpet. His eyes was sunk back in his head behind a pair of horn-rimmed spectacles and he had a scraggly mustache that sort of wrapped around his mouth. But he was wearin' a smile and a fancy dress uniform with lots of gold braid and big gold buttons. And he was smokin' a big cigar.

Four-Mile was speechless. His eyes were just about ready to roll out on the carpet.

"Meet the man who has given me true love," Annie said with a flourish. "My husband and the master of the *New Union Victory*, Captain Reginald Glendenning."

Epilogue

The end came in 1915 when the Ottumwa
Belle, *under Capt. Walter L. Hunter, brought
the last tow of logs down the Mississippi....
When he died at Bellevue, Iowa, in 1962,
ninety-four years old, diesels had prodded
steamboats off the river. But the old whistles
and raftsman's cry echoed in his memory.*
—Walter Havighurst

JUNE 22, 1881:

I'm way behind keepin' this log and I feel bad about it. But
when you're flat on your back you don't get much done. For a
long time I had those nightmares most every night and they was
always the same: I'd see flames shootin' in the air and I'd try to
swim but I couldn't. But I'm sleepin' better now. Much better.

I still think about the *Jessie Bill* a lot and sometimes it's extra
hard to keep the tears back. Everythin' was goin' good for us
early in the season and we must've set some kind of a record,
makin' three trips to Beef Slough without any real trouble.
Maybe that was the problem: things was too good.

I keep tellin' myself it wasn't anybody's fault. If the river
stage had been right and if the night had been clear, it never
would've happened. But we'd had several days of nothin' but
rain and the river was high and mean, too. It made me think of
that wild trip when we took the lumber raft to Grafton. I noticed

there was some fog when we went into Crooked Slough below Lansing, but after that I don't remember much.

Some say the *Colonel Davenport* had too big a raft for that kind of water. Maybe, maybe not. But when it broke up, it filled up the whole channel and the *Jessie Bill* never had a chance. There was no way Wabasha Dan could've seen those two big brails comin' at him. All of a sudden I was in the water and I was plenty scared, even after Four-Mile got me by the collar.

When you get run over by a raft, there ain't much left, let me tell you. The firebox flew open when we turned over and it wasn't long until the whole mess was on fire. I guess that was good because it gave a little light when the *Davenport* started fishin' us out of the river.

Cap'n Lafe and Wabasha Dan never made it. It was several days before they found 'em. I think about all the terrible things I used to say about poor ol' Lafe, and Dan, too, and I hope the Good Lord will forgive me, because I miss 'em both. And I miss Grumble Jones, too. They got him out, but he was hurt bad and he only lived two or three days.

I wouldn't want you to think I'm feelin' sorry for myself. My busted leg is comin' along good and I'm spending most of my time at Van Sant's Boatyard. Professor Howe had no trouble at all raisin' the money to build a new boat. She's gonna be a fine one and we should have her in the water in another month or so.

Four-Mile, he'll be the captain and Cleve will do the pilotin'. He's due to take his examination at Rock Island next week. Pot Belly has decided to retire and Mudcat Lewis wants to be the engineer. Limber Jim Gray will take over as first mate and I agreed to stay on as mud clerk, as long as I can work a little as steersman and don't have to cook. If I stay with it, I think I can get my pilot's license in two years.

Folks keep askin' if we've got a name for the new boat and I tell 'em that took less than a minute. She's the *Jessie Bill II*. What else?

I don't want everybody to know it, but I'm courtin' Petunia some, when I have a little extra time. Nothin' serious, you understand. I guess she's learned a lot lately, because I can tell she's a heap smarter. And another funny thing: she's not half as homely as she used to be.